Curtis Dunham

The Casino Girl in London

By herself

Curtis Dunham

The Casino Girl in London
By herself

ISBN/EAN: 9783337428938

Printed in Europe, USA, Canada, Australia, Japan

Cover: Foto ©Andreas Hilbeck / pixelio.de

More available books at **www.hansebooks.com**

THE CASINO GIRL
IN LONDON

BY

HERSELF

EDITED BY CURTIS DUNHAM

(*Illustrated*)

R. F. FENNO & COMPANY, 9 AND 11 EAST
SIXTEENTH STREET : : NEW YORK
1898

Contents

"They never proceed to follow that Light,
But always follow me."
—*The Belle of New York.*

CHAPTER I

I HAD just finished dressing for the second act and was applying to my lips those touches of rouge which give them their demure expression, when there came a tap on my dressing-room door.

"If it is Lord Dangerford, Prue," said I, "thank him for the tiger's skin and say that I'll be at home to-morrow at three."

"Lord Dangerford be blowed," said a familiar voice the moment Prue had opened the door. And then the voice continued: "Are you presentable? May we come in?"

The voice belonged to the American Friend —a most accommodating and useful person. So I replied in accents as amiable as I could command under the circumstances—a foggy first act blighted by a dull tea at the Honorable Mrs. Pebblestone's:

"Come in; I'll give you just two minutes— and the tip is tuppence."

9

"I say, really, talking of tips, you'll be surprised, you know."

This remark proceeded from Squibs, of the *Gazette*, a nice sort of chap, one of the first, in fact, to predict for me the flattering social success in London which was so soon to be realized. I shook hands with Squibs.

"Mr. Squibs is right," said the American Friend. "You will be surprised. We are here to tip you, but not with tuppence, my dear."

"'Arf a crown goes 'ere, sir," chimed in Little Bobby, appearing from behind the broad shoulders of the American Friend. "I say, Miss Casino, lend me a needle and a bit of thread. My—ahem—arum-a-tum-tums caught on a nail, and the Censor's in front. Evening, Squibsey. You're looking out of sight. When do I get that notice?"

Little Bobby is not responsible. But she is pretty and clever, and so we bear with her. At a sign from me Prue took her behind a screen, from whence occasional shrieks announced plainly enough that the needle was doing its work.

"What is this extraordinary tip you're so excited about?" I asked, as I made a last dab into the rouge pot. "Not the races. I warn you, never again the races. Not to be flippant, there are two things I shall always remember: first, the Maine; second, the Ascot Cup. With respect to the latter, my dressmaker and a certain worthy greengrocer with a growing family are my comrades in adversity. If it is the races, good evening."

"On the contrary, it's a sure thing," said the American Friend.

"Exactly what the welcher said about his tip on the Cup," said I.

"Squibs, you tell her," said the American Friend; "my clothes still seem to smell of that beastly race."

The journalist beamed upon me again.

"It's something awfully jolly, you know, Miss Casino. You are to write a book."

"I beg your pardon, Mr. Squibs?"

"I say, old chap, you tell her," said Squibs, who seemed disconcerted by my evident incredulity.

"That's perfectly straight," said the American Friend; "you are to write a book about your London experiences."

"Who is foolish enough to want to read about my London experiences?" I demanded.

" The American public, my dear; the great American public."

" And the London public. 'Pon honor, the London public would be charmed, you know," said Squibs.

" But what experiences have I had that people would care to read about?" I asked, still more than half believing that the American Friend was chaffing me.

"Rubbish!" piped Little Bobby over the screen. "Did you meet the Prince, or didn't you?"

Whereat Mr. Squibs nodded his head, still smiling reassuringly.

"Do you mean that I could do that without exhibiting vulgar disrespect? How could I go about boasting of such things—least of all put them into a book?"

" Oh, really, now, you know," said Mr. Squibs, "that's all your American idea. It depends on how it's done."

" Exactly," said the American Friend. " Why half the country inns in England are patronized by the royal family, if you may believe their advertisements."

" And I wash with the same soap the Queen

does," chirped Little Bobby; "it says so on the box."

And Mr. Squibs, the best mannered and best dressed man I had met in England, sat and smiled and nodded his head as much as to say : " You see how we do it over here, my dear. It is little things like these that have made us the greatest nation that ever ruled the earth. Why can't you take a leaf out of our book, Miss Casino ? When you are in Rome—you know the rest."

"First of all you owe it to your profession at home," said the American Friend, " to write this book."

"What interest has my profession at home in the matter," I asked, "besides its natural joy at the spectacle of a fellow member making a fool of herself? "

This rude inquiry seemed to put the American Friend on his mettle, and he proceeded to argue the matter, with a certain logic, I must admit, as follows :

"My dear, you're too modest. You don't half appreciate the significance of your achievement. It was reserved for you to turn the tide of conquest. For how many years had that tide flowed uninterruptedly from East to West—

from London to New York? Consider the long procession beginning with the original British Blonde "—

"Oh Lord! the British Blonde!" sniffed Little Bobby, behind the screen.

"And ending with the Gaiety Girl."

"The girl we've left behind us," commented Little Bobby with unction.

"Always moving with the Sun from East to West. My dear, is it nothing to have headed a procession that moves in the opposite direction? To have represented your profession with distinction? To have compelled the leaders of society "—

"Not forgetting 'Is Royal 'Ighness," said Little Bobby, grasping another opportunity to practise her brand new cockney dialect.

"To open their doors to you? Is such a conquest to go unchronicled merely because its heroine has scruples about exploiting herself in the light of attentions paid her by Lord Dangerford, the Marquis of Silsbury, and one who "—

"Oh, I'll answer for the Prince," said Little Bobby, cheerfully; "he'll be tickled to death."

"Really, Miss Casino, the matter doesn't admit of argument, you know," urged Mr. Squibs.

"But I don't know the first thing about writing a book," I protested. "It is one thing to sit down and write to a friend about your experiences, and quite another to put them into a book for everybody to read. I shouldn't know how to begin, even. Perhaps if I could imagine that I were whispering my confidences into the ear of a discreet and loyal friend in America "—

Another interruption from Little Bobby, who now appeared from behind the screen with her garb repaired and her shapely limbs fit for the Managerial Censor's most critical scrutiny.

"The Statue of Liberty," she said, with a triumphant glance at Mr. Squibs.

"Bravo!" exclaimed that gentleman, clapping his gloved hands. "I say, Miss Casino, there's an idea for you. It makes all plain sailing, with opportunity for a genuine Homeric touch at the beginning of the first chapter."

"For example?" said I, insinuatingly. And Mr. Squibs rose and declaimed my first chapter in this wise:

"Into your ear, O chaste and beneficent Goddess, I venture to whisper these confessions. Since last I saw you, draped in your classic robes, bearing aloft your steadfast torch, no triumph won in a strange land has driven from my memory the smile of encouragement which I seemed to see hovering upon thy chiseled lips. It was that smile, O Liberty, that revived my drooping spirits; that bade me resign myself with confidence to the good ship, to the venerable ocean, and to the arms of the mother country.   Therefore, dear Goddess, when, in my crude and untutored way,"—

"Tommy rot!" broke in Little Bobby. "Chuck it."

"Second act!" yelled the call boy, thrusting his head into my dressing-room.

"So be it," I said, as Mr. Squibs escaped with the American Friend.   "But 'my crude and untutored way' shall speak for itself without apology."

And so the die was cast.

CHAPTER II

"My dear, do be calm," said the Artiste, who, swaddled like a mummy in her Scotch plaid steamer rug, was placidly reading a French novel. "Sit down. Be quiet. You'll annoy the Captain. He knows what he's about."

"It's all very well for you who have crossed before," I said, "to have confidence in the Captain. As for me, I think I know how to sympathize with Columbus' poor sailors. Here we have been for six days floating about in a fog. We are supposed to be somewhere in the English Channel. Yesterday we were promised a glimpse of Scilly. Last night we were to have seen the Lizzard light, but didn't. I have faith to believe that when we lost sight of Sandy Hook the Captain had aimed the ship for that fly speck off somewhere beyond the Northeastern horizon called England, but what assurance have I that he'll hit the mark? I don't blame the Captain. It's a mighty small mark to hit in a fog."

17

The last words of my plaint were drowned in the groaning shriek of the siren. Presently there came an answering groan, faint but ominous, from somewhere off the port bow—the first we had heard since our ship's dismal solo began off the Banks.

"Cheer up," said the Artiste, closing her novel and preparing to emerge from her rug.

"Does that mean land?" I asked eagerly.

Again our siren spoke, and its voice seemed to have an upward inflection. Again came the answering groan, louder and with a menacing note in it.

"It means a ship crossing our bows."

"A companion in misery is something," I said.

The dialogue between the two sirens was becoming rapid and emphatic. We stood by the rail straining our eyes to catch a glimpse of the stranger through the swirling mist. Little Bobby, her tossing curls beady with moisture, came flying toward us from the door of the wheel house.

"Buck up, me 'earties," exclaimed our industrious imitator of the cockney Second Steward. "Hit's only two hours to Southampton."

"How do you know?" I asked.

"The First Hofficer just said so."

"How does the First Officer know?"

"'E says as 'ow the other boat is a French packet making for Jersey."

"Then but for the fog we should be within sight of the Isle of Wight," I said. "Oh what a beastly entrance!"

I had set my heart on a more propitious approach to the scene of the conquest expected of me. The gloomy passage had intensified all the superstitions of ,my profession. I trembled at the thought of the opening night in London —London! The name of this centre of the theatrical universe seemed to gain new dignity from my present standpoint. I, a miserable atom tossed by wretched little Channel waves, buried in a fog, crawling blindly toward the giant to seize him for my prey! Already tremors of stage fright were shaking my poor knees. An effective entrance upon the scene is half the battle. Would that first terrible London audience be frozen into indifference by an entrance upon the stage as wretched as that I was now making upon England? What a dreadful omen! Oh, that the fog would lift; oh, for a single ray of sunlight!

"How are you feeling, dear?" It was the

Comédienne, the maddest, merriest, most irresponsible of our party. Her expression was woe-begone. The light had gone out of her eyes. Her nose was red. She rubbed it on my shoulder tearfully as she put her arm around me and snuggled up as though to a natural protector.

"Goodness gracious, go away!" I exclaimed. "You are free enough with your pranks when the sun shines. Now that a little artificial warmth would be appreciated you are as limp as a rag. Go away; I hate red noses in a fog."

"Very well, dear. I knew it. You feel just as I do, and I feel just as that prince of bluffers, Monte Cristo, looks from the front as though he must feel when he stands on the rock in his rags and shouts like an idiot: 'The world is mine!' Darling, I want to go home."

To cap the climax of our misery Daffy came up leaning tenderly on the arm of the Liar. They had been sworn enemies for months. Now her dank hair brushed his cheek, and they leaned upon each other for support in their despair. Little Bobby, dancing up, broke the spell.

"Buck up, me boy," she said to the Liar,

giving him a slap on the back. "The bloomin' ship's still afloat."

"Look! the fog is lifting," I exclaimed, as the shadowy form of the other ship hove in sight a quarter of a mile away, having crossed our course.

"The Sun! the Sun!" said the Comédienne.

Far behind us the dull sea gleamed with a touch of silver. It looked like a patch the size of a city square. It seemed to be overtaking us. A glorious acre of blue smiled above it. The banks of fog rolled back still farther. The rent in the clouds broadened. The patch of silver danced forward and enveloped us.

"Hip, hip!" said the Comédienne. "Hurrah for us!"

The sound of angry, sarcastic voices reached me. Daffy and the Liar had resumed their feud.

"How dare you speak to me, sir!"

"Excuse me for being alive?"

In front of us the horizon was still blurred by misty clouds. I searched eagerly among them for outlines more stable than their changing shapes. My eyes were keen for the first sight of land. My eyesight is famously good. It had already given odds to several glasses ostentatiously carried about by fellow passengers. I said to myself that if I could be the first to discern the Needles and their neighboring white cliffs all the bad omens of the voyage would go for nought. I should accept the new augury as a foretaste of victory over there a little way beyond the misty clouds. I was conscious of a powerful attraction in the ship that had crossed our course almost at right angles. She seemed to be proceeding with a confidence that we somehow lacked. I glanced at the bridge and saw the Captain scanning a wide expanse of the horizon with his glass. "Is he looking for a pilot?" I asked myself. "Or is he in doubt about his course?" Even idiots find short cuts to the truth. I could not help feeling that we were sailing too much toward the East. So I continued to bend my gaze in the direction of the stranger ship, past her deep into the mist that each moment grew more diaphanous as the rays of the afternoon sun became warmer and more penetrating. Presently certain clouds appeared to me to take on the quality of a veil swaying over rugged outlines that were immovable. I rubbed my eyes and looked again. No. I was not mistaken. Something solid was behind that veil.

It was land—the first foreign shore I had ever beheld.

"It's mine, mine!" I cried joyfully.

"What's yours?" queried a chorus of voices.

"England, London," said I.

"And pray why is England yours?" inquired the Artiste regarding me with amazement.

"Because I saw it first," said I.

"Oh, that settles it," said the Comédienne. "But where?"

"The other ship is making straight for it."

"I see nothing but clouds," said the Artiste, turning away. "The nearest land must be the Isle of Wight, and if the Isle of Wight lies over there what in the name of goodness are we steering for?"

A profane exclamation from the Liar directed our attention to a new phenomenon. He was leaning over the rail and apostrophizing our ship's wake, which was curving like a rainbow.

"Look!" I cried in triumph. "We are turning toward the North. We are following the other ship. What did I tell you?"

My triumph was complete. Our ship completed a sweeping semicircle and then headed straight for the white cliffs that now showed distinctly in the sun, all but their summits which were wreathed in a film of vapor.

When we had finished dancing about the deck and hugging each other, Little Bobby approached me with exaggerated humility, her forefinger at the side of her bicycle cap, and said:

" Hi begs yer pardon, missus; Hengland is yours.   Hi 'ereby renounces hall claim."

Followed by the Comédienne praying:

" Please, mum, all I asks is one little Duke."

" My dears, if Dukes are to be had for the asking each of you shall go home a Duchess. At this moment I feel that London is already mine. You may have the Dukes and welcome."

To me these details of first impressions are not trivial or unworthy of a place in this chronicle. All of them had a significant bearing upon the momentous object of my pilgrimage. London, presented to my mind's eye lurking behind a rampart of fog, seemed a monster crouching in ambush eager to crush and devour me. It did not seem to me that I could survive a landing on English soil under such malevolent conditions. The coming of the sun, the glistening welcome of Britain's white cliffs,

" Dancing about the deck.''—Page 24.

changed all. London and that crucial first
night lost all their terrors. As the red-tiled
roofs came into view beyond the white cliffs,
and the sweet English landscape, with its
charming richness of verdure, seemed to smile
upon me with a countenance clean and glowing
as though just washed by heaven in honor of
my coming, I had a prophetic vision of my first
London audience showering upon me its favors
from boxes, stalls, pit and gallery. At that
moment I knew the vision would be realized.
And though I knew it would have faded away
hours before my great need of it should come I
was grateful for it, and I kissed my hands at
the green hedges and the close, dark foliage
again and again.

Up the Solent, past Cowes where the towers
of Osborne House, beloved of the Queen, point
their fingers upward through green domes, on
past gently sloping hillsides checkered with
different-hued crops, lights and shadows playing hide and seek everywhere, their outlines
softened and vague in the humid atmosphere.
Yes. This was the England of my dreams.
Who would not die fighting for her?—Who of
her sons? Who could hope to wrest her from

them? Shade of Julius Cæsar, what were you thinking of?

Evidences of an unusual commotion about the decks disturbed my reverie. A donkey engine awoke into spasmodic industry. Excited voices reached my ears.

"Little Bobby! Little Bobby!"

"Comin', mum, comin'."

"Look, Little Bobby. Coming through the gate. Your namesake."

We were within a stone's throw of the Southampton Docks, and the Comédienne had caught sight of a burly and awesome figure surmounted by a black helmet strapped under his moustache. He raised an authoritative forefinger and an obstreperous cart horse reared back on his haunches, saluting with his forefeet in the air, and instantly became meek and law-abiding.

Safely landed. Special train for London waiting in the background. Money changer in foreground doing a rushing business. Hand over known value in Uncle Sam's pledges to redeem; receive unknown value in coins bearing Her Majesty's portrait. Pocketbook stuffed with them. They must be good for everybody wants a sample. Porters on all sides, smiling and expectant.

"Boxes, mum? This way, mum. Thank you." Two and six.

"Customs hofficer? Division C, mum. Thank you." Two bob.

"Cable hoffice, mum? First turn on the left, mum. Thank you." One and six.

"Change for a sovereign, mum? Hover by the door, mum. Thank you." Threppence— all the coppers in my purse.

"Luggage to London, mum? This way, mum. Thank you." One bob.

"Check for luggage, mum? An Hamerican custom, mum. Quite superfluous 'ere, mum. Thank you." Sixpence.

"First class carriage, mum? 'Ere you are, mum. Thank you." Tuppence.

"Compartment hexclusive, mum? Difficult, mum—thank you (half a crown)—but possible. 'Ere you are, mum. Thank you." Two shillings.

The Comédienne is flushed and disheveled. She throws herself back in a corner of the compartment, breathing hard.

"My dear, have you any of those portraits of the Queen left in your purse?"

" A few.   Why do you ask ? "

" Lend me tuppence, won't you.   I have a presentiment that the Prince will be at the station."

Rumble and roar.   More green hedges; more red tiled roofs.   It is nearly nine o'clock, but the sky is still red over the hills to the Northwest.   The long English Spring twilight has just begun.   It still lingers while we rattle through the tawdry modern suburbs of the giant city.   Cheap new brick boxes only a trifle smaller than the squalid, vainglorious " gardens" which contain them.   All the charm of rural England has vanished.   All the majesty of London's ancient history is insulted and dimmed by this plebeian, upstart approach. My recent vision of certain, speedy conquest has faded quite away.   Grey old St. Paul's to the right; Westminster and the Houses of Parliament on the left.   Once more I am a wretched atom, the sport of destiny.

London—Waterloo Station. " Alone in London ! "

CHAPTER III

A SMALL residential hotel at the bottom of some fag end of a street near the Strand which I never could find without the assistance of a policeman, sheltered me during my first week in London. The establishment had a meek and brow-beaten exterior wholly inconsistent with its inner workings. A "residential" hotel in London is a hotel that provides all the discomforts of home and presents an itemized bill for the same at the end of each week. The bill includes "attendance," but that fact, stipulated in the bond, does not absolve you from the foreigner's sacred duty of scattering his small change right and left, morning, noon and night. As he sows silver and coppers so shall he reap the necessaries of existence. No planting of the seed, no harvesting of the crop. Fortunately for my physical comfort I was far too depressed mentally to make any show of resistance. I was a veritable fountain designed for no other apparent purpose than that of spouting a steady stream of coin of the realm, which, descending in a spray of shillings and sixpence, should moisten the parched palms of the serving multitude. Though I must admit that the greater part of this multitude was distinguished by a rugged and constitutional honesty in most matters, my entire willingness to accept ten shillings in change for a sovereign and an equal number of pennies for a shilling, was a source of no small profit to numerous worthy persons.

Three horrible days and nights had to be lived through before I should know my fate. Between showers on the afternoon of the first day I set out for a stroll to the theatre, barely half a dozen squares distant on the other side of the Strand, intending to inspect the line of distinguished Londoners awaiting their turn at the box office, and to determine, if possible, to what extent the royal family and the nobility were represented. After losing myself seven or eight times, and each time being assured by a policeman that "the first turning to the right, second turning to the left " would bring me to my destination, I secured a hansom, and, having been driven at least six miles in as many different directions—for which I had to pay eight miles' worth—I was at length deposited in front of a large frame of photographs exhibiting my attractions in different costumes.

Alas! in vain I looked for that long line of prospective first-nighters representing the flower of British aristocracy. The box office was there. Its window stood invitingly open. A gentleman with a beard, a high forehead and an aspect of congealed expectancy stared into the deserted lobby through the aperture. On either side of the entrance fulsome announcements of my coming, of my astonishing and overpowering gifts, of my high personal and artistic excellencies too numerous to mention, stared me in the face like hollow mockeries.

Presently two unclean youths smoking pipes stopped in front of the photographs, looked them over in contemptuous silence, and passed on to one of the bills, which they proceeded with much deliberation to read and digest. Finally the more unclean of the two remarked:

"W'ot do you s'y, Bill?"

"Gammon, I says."

"Cheek, says I."

And they went on their way puffing at their pipes.

Scorned by the pit. Held in contempt by the gallery. What could I expect from the stalls? Would the boxes deign to recognize the fact of my existence?

So I called another hansom and drove dismally back to my sowing of shillings and my reaping of small civilities.

Domiciled with me during these days of supreme trial were the Artiste, the Comédienne, Little Bobby, Daffy, the Liar, and Tommy Atkins—the last so named on account of her instantly acquired propensity for running after the Queen's scarlet-coated protectors. The Artiste wore her customary air of serenity. The others might have been festooned with crape and gained thereby no added aspect of woe.

The state apartments of the establishment, consisting of a sitting-room and, presumably, a sleeping-room, were directly across the narrow hall from my own comparatively humble quarters. They were occupied by that mighty personage, our manager, who was booked to sail for America on the Saturday after our opening. His efforts to appear smiling and confident were really pitiful. Fortunately a cosmopolitan individual, hardened by many years of managerial controversies with Italian prima donna and French tragediennes on land and sea—a veritable singed cat among managers—widely known as "the American's Friend in London," called daily with words of hope. Accordingly our manager was enabled to pull himself together when in our presence and maintain a mild and uncertain semblance of authority. On the morning of the day of our opening performance I chanced to discover how really desperate was the situation which confronted him. A chambermaid entering with a shilling's worth of inquiry whether I had rung, and making her mollified exit leaving the door ajar, I was startled by the sound of violent weeping which seemed to come from across the hall. I stepped outside my door and perceived that the lamentations proceeded from our manager's sitting-room, his door being slightly open. Mingled with these mournful sounds were indistinct ejaculations of protest. The latter at length gained the ascendancy, and my astonished ears drank in the following significant words:

"No, no; I say no. You shall stay. You shall not go back with me. I tell you I shall not trust Miss Casino to the tender mercies of a lot of envious English chorus people. Now my dear, do brace up."

"Boo, hoo, hoo, I don't care; I want to go home. Boo, hoo, hoo, hoo."

It was Little Bobby. I could hardly believe my ears. At the manager's next words I nearly fainted.

"Little Bobby, you are the limit. I thought I could rely on you. I expected it of the others, and I haven't been disappointed. They've all been here begging me to take them home, throwing away the opportunity of their lives, weeping buckets full—every one of them. But you, I "—

I waited to hear no more, but returned to my room and proceeded to weep several buckets full on my own account. I had hardly accomplished this comforting duty when the Comédienne burst into my room in a state of wild dismay, crying:

"It's all over."

I gave her a look of resigned inquiry.

"London won't have us. It's all settled."

And then, flinging herself into an armchair and swaying to and fro distractedly, the Comédienne uttered these ominous words:

"Daffy and the Liar are making up again!"

I have already mentioned the brief suspension of this celebrated feud during the darkest period of our foggy approach to England. It was well understood among us that the mildest approach to an armistice between these two mortal enemies portended calamity. The fact that they were actually making up was pregnant with the most disastrous possibilities. The Comédienne and I sat staring at each other in stony despair until we were summoned to attend the final dress rehearsal.

I have prayed that this humiliating function might be erased from my memory. Chaos is the only word that approaches an intelligent description of it. To begin with, the manager worked himself into a violent temper over the absence of one of the scene shifters. Then he created a panic among the chorus people by sending them all to their rooms to dress over again. There was a tempest over a wrinkle in one of the Artiste's first act stockings, from which that usually placid person retired in tears. My make-up was declared to have been applied with a whitewash brush, whereat I wept and spent another half hour over it. It was after four o'clock when the company's outward aspect finally passed muster. But there was worse to come.

"Now if you will condescend to give me a part—only a part—of your valuable attention," said the manager, with withering courtesy, "I desire to make a few general remarks—pertinent, I assure you, and necessary.   Is there any one present who knows how it seems to play to empty benches?"

A moment of silence relieved by scattering spasmodic sobs.

"Does it happen that any of you know what it is to be hissed?"

More sobs interspersed with sundry gulps and moans.

"Perchance a few of you know how it feels to be pelted with cabbages—and other vegetables?"

Whimpers from the ladies; sepulchral groans from the gentlemen.

"Fie, fie, ladies and gentlemen.   At your ages—I believe some of you ladies are more than sixteen—to still cherish such childish illusions—always packed houses, always applause and curtain calls, always bouquets and bracelets.   Fie, fie, I say."

And then, after a ghastly pause, in tones of thunder:

"Have any of you ever had to WALK HOME!"

Sounds of lamentation from all sides.   Above which, in still more thunderous accents:

"It is well. This night shall bring to you the blessing of wisdom. The house will be empty. You will be hissed. You will be pelted with cabbages. And to-morrow "—

Another tragic pause.

"TO-MORROW YOU WALK HOME!"

Whereupon Daffy and the Liar instantly and publicly fell into each other's arms.

The rehearsal then proceeded with tolerable success. Chastened by mental suffering, resigned to the worst, we were martyrs to duty, going through our parts with a precision never before achieved.

At the conclusion of the rehearsal the manager looked at his watch, smiled the smile of a victorious general and said:

"Seven o'clock. I have ordered some tea and buttered buns served on the stage. Any member of the company removing his or her costume or make-up until after this evening's performance will be fined one week's salary. Jack! Jack!"

The guardian of the stage entrance appeared.

"Jack, lock the doors."

We will pass over the interval of tea and buttered buns.

It was perhaps an hour later, while I was

nervously experimenting with my darkened eye-lashes, that the Comédienne burst into my dressing-room wildly excited, saying:

"What do you think, dear? There are at least fifty people in the gallery!" And out she bounded again.

This was the signal for a succession of start-ling communications hurled at me through my open door during the next half hour.

"Well, if this 'ere ain't a rum go. The pit is packed," screamed Little Bobby at me with sparkling eyes.

"The stalls are filling up," shrieked Tommy Atkins.

"Such swells you never saw," added the Comédienne.

"They make a New York first night audi-ence look like tuppence ha'penny," declared Lit-tle Bobby.

And then a succession of duets, trios, quar-tettes and choruses:

"The stalls are full. Hooray!"

"The gallery is jammed."

"Gee! Even the boxes are sold!"

"But not occupied this early!" I exclaimed, starting incredulously for the peep hole.

But even before I beheld the crowded house

waiting impatiently for the curtain to rise I saw that which stilled all my fears.

Daffy and the Liar were scowling at each other from opposite sides of the stage. They had resumed their feud.

When I turned in amazement from the peep hole I found the American Friend at my side.

"Not a bad house," said he, calmly.

"If only it was money," I sighed.

"What else could it be?" he asked in evident surprise.

"Paper," I said; "paper to save appearances."

"Nonsense. It's pounds, shillings and pence, with the accent on the pounds, my dear."

"But the boxes"—

"Oh, Lord Dangerford, having just returned from his annual quest of big game in the jungle, has a very natural zest for civilized amusements. As for the Honorable Mrs. Pebblestone"—

"The Honorable Mrs. Pebblestone here?" I exclaimed, doubting the evidence of my ears.

"Certainly. Her party occupies two boxes. She is an ardent patron of the stage, you know. That accounts for her early arrival."

I had not dared to hope for this. I had already learned of the powerful influence exerted by this lady in London society, and had wondered how it would seem if a miracle should enable me to appear before her.

"Of course it will be a little late before all the boxes are filled," continued the American Friend. "The Duchess of Edgecombe rarely reaches the theatre before nine or half past, and you can't count on Lady Dunstable, Countess Pipedreme or the Earl of Drippingeaves much before that hour.

"Do you mean that all these have taken boxes?" I demanded in astonishment.

"Certainly. Why not? It isn't every day the Casino Girl comes to London."

I ran back to my room with my senses all awhirl. The overture was ended. A burst of applause from the gallery informed me that the curtain was up. I seemed to hear vaguely from a distance the first lines of the opening chorus:

> When a man is twenty-one
> Let him drink hot rum;
> Let him drink it hot and cold—
> Hot and cold.

Then I pulled myself together, feeling my cheeks burn at the sudden recollection that I,

" Ze lady from France, she walk like zis."—Page 41.

an independent American girl, was allowing
my head to be turned by the prospect of presently attracting the notice of half a dozen pairs
of aristocratic eyes. Soon another sentiment,
even more powerful, enlivened all my faculties. I could hear the Artiste, in her precise
manner, giving the exact shade of meaning to
each line, singing:

> Ze American girl she walk like zis
>   Iu a haughty mannaire,
> Ze lady from France she walk like zis
>   Iu a naughty mannaire.
> Now which do you like ze best, M'sieur?
> Now which do you like to see,
> Ze 'aughty proud American girl
> Or ze lady from gay Paree?

I left my room and stood in the wings while
the song continued. I could see white gloved
hands leveling lorgnettes upon the singer, in
the boxes opposite. In stalls, pit and gallery
there were characteristic evidences of admiring attention. It was plain that the Artiste
was making herself popular. I had been told
that an encore was proof of extraordinary favor
with a London audience, and here was I having that record made for me to beat at the very
start!

It is enough for me to say that the Artiste's example was not wasted on the Salvation Lassie. In my first song there is this quatrain:

> And I therefore cannot see,
> When I go out to preach,
> Why men must say to me
> That I'm a perfect peach.

Advised by the management I emphasized slightly the word "peach," and not without a favorable result, as the sequel will show.

The curtain had hardly fallen on the first act when a note was delivered to me in my dressing-room which read as follows:

"Lord Dangerford presents his compliments and requests Miss Casino to reply by the bearer defining the word, 'Peach,' as used in her charming song."

My reply written on the same sheet was this:

"Miss Casino begs to inform Lord Dangerford that the word, 'Peach,' as used in the song, is an Americanism signifying that the object to which it is applied is entitled to the superlative degree of respectful admiration."

The second act was no less successful than the first. On returning to my dressing-room at its close I found two notes awaiting me. The first ran thus:

"Mr. Squibs, of the *Gazette*, presents his compliments and begs that Miss Casino will accept his assurances of the unanimous and cordial commendation of the London press."

I may remark here that Mr. Squibs' assurances proved perfectly trustworthy.

The other note—which contained an odd-shaped bit of dull metal heavily mounted in gold with a few links of gold chain attached to it—read as follows:

"Lord Dangerford begs to assure Miss Casino that he considers her a large basket of peaches, and requests her to accept as a souvenir of this occasion the bullet with which he shot and killed his first elephant."

CHAPTER IV

SEATED in a golden chariot drawn by four beautiful pale blue horses in ecru trappings, I was bowing and smiling right and left to the cheering multitude while approaching the purple draped dais upon which stood a majestic figure in a great iron grey horsehair wig making obeisances innumerable in my direction and extending politely the handle of a gigantic iron key, when I felt myself suddenly seized by some rude hand while a shrill voice cried, as the multitude, the golden chariot, the ecru-trapped blue horses and the gentleman with the big iron key seemed to fade away:

"Do wake up, my dear. Wake up. Wake up!"

It was the Comédienne with an armful of newspapers skaking me violently by the shoulder.

"There, at last! My dear, you left a call

44

for ten o'clock, and here it is nearly noon.
What is the matter? Are you ill?"

"No, dear, not ill," I replied, drowsily;
"only dreaming."

"Well, you don't need to dream any more,"
and the Comédienne threw down the newspapers on the foot of my bed.

"I was sitting in a golden chariot surrounded by the cheering populace and the Lord
Mayor in a big wig was just about to present
me with the keys of London, when"—

"Never mind, dear," interrupted the Comédienne, as she complacently marked an article
in one of the papers with a blue pencil, "the
keys of London, figuratively speaking, have
been delivered according to the modern custom
while the person thus honored was still sleep-
ing. Here they are." And the Comédienne
buried me beneath a rustling coverlet of complimentary press notices. "How could you
sleep until you knew what the critics thought
about it?"

"Mr. Squibs, of the *Gazette*, sent me a note
last night assuring me of the hearty commendation of the entire London press."

"And you could go to sleep like a baby on
the strength of that?" The Comédienne re-

garded me with admiring eyes. "Your faith is something most gorgeous and beautiful to behold."

"You don't mean," said I in sudden alarm, reaching for one of the papers, "that Mr. Squibs "—

"No," laughed the Comédienne, "I don't mean that Mr. Squibs' judgment was warped by the spell cast over him by the Casino Girl. He is a true prophet. The notices are all like the one you have in your hand—nearly a column each in which they declare unanimously that London is yours."

I turned my attention to the coffee and rolls which arrived at this juncture, remarking, after a moment, to the Comédienne, who was still making ecstatic blue pencil commentaries:

"My dear, I've a notion to go out and view my new possessions."

"Splendid idea. May I go with you? Shall I call a brougham?"

"No, not a brougham. I shall view the West End at another time, under auspices as flattering as they are appropriate. In fact Lord Dangerford "—

"What! Already?" said the Comédienne. "When I left the theatre last night there wasn't a single Johnny at the stage door—not that it makes any difference to me," she added, hastily, "but since you mention his Lordship,"—

"When you have looked about you a little more," I said, composedly, "you will learn that the nobility enjoy certain privileges which ordinary members of the aristocracy do not. Stage door civilities, for example, while including such diversions as excursions by private launch up the Thames, coaching parties to Richmond and Hampton Court, besides more Bohemian recreations which I prefer not to discuss—stage door civilities, I repeat, may have an aristocratic origin which members of the chorus"—

"If you've been reading Baedeker of course I've nothing more to say," broke in the Comédienne, in the jerky manner customary with her when she is not wholly pleased with the outlook.

"I was about to refer," I resumed, calmly, "to certain correspondence between my dressing-room and one of the boxes after the first act last night,"—

"It's against the rules of the management," snapped the Comédienne.

"My dear, you are yet to learn that in Lon-

don managers of theatres make rules for the
benefit of the chorus.   With respect to the—er
—I may say the prima donna, and members of
the nobility, all rules, as well as all bets, are
off.   I shall not attempt to conceal from you,
dear, that the correspondence of which I spoke
was with Lord Dangerford.   You will find a
specimen of it on my dressing table, I think—
there, to the right, the extremely bad hand
writing, under the gold mounted bullet with
which his Lordship killed his first elephant.
Oh, certainly, read it, if you like."

There is a certain class of girls who go upon
the stage, girls of extraordinary animal spirits
and ambition, with whom one has to be a little
high-handed occasionally.   Otherwise the world
would be full of prima donnas and business at
a standstill for lack of choruses.   I am sorry to
say that the Comédienne, otherwise a most
charming companion, belongs to this class.   Of
course, strictly speaking, she is one of the prin-
cipals of the company; but after all there are
really only two general classifications, and I
have always felt it my duty to the management
to curb any tendency toward forgetfulness of
this fact.

" Very well," said the Comédienne, making

an effort not to appear sulky, "then I'll call a hansom."

"Don't trouble yourself, dear," I replied amiably; "I'm not going to St. John's Wood, to-day. I shall probably take a house there presently, but to-day I shall view my new possessions, the City of London, appropriately, in a 'bus, wearing my oldest boots, my white cotton stockings and my most dilapidated hat. I hope I'm patriotic and all that, but I hate to be pointed at wherever I go as an American just arrived. My dear, you are altogether too neatly and becomingly dressed ever to be in the swim in London."

"If it is necessary to be a dowdy to be in the swim in London, then I prefer to stand on my record as an American," said the Comédienne, defiantly. "I shan't change a thing."

It was a charming morning when I raised the blind and looked out. It hadn't rained for fifteen minutes, and there were indications that another half hour would elapse before the natives would begin to shudder over prospects of a dry season. So we lost no time in setting out. We walked up the Strand to Trafalgar Square for a starting point. This and St. Paul's are the only two localities in London from which I have ever made a successful start for anywhere else. We were speedily discovered, and no less promptly classified as to nationality in spite of my white cotton stockings, by a policeman who had not yet been lured by the fickle sun to remove his waterproof cape. He held up an inquiring forefinger. Whereat we made a frantic scramble through the billows of vehicles of all kinds toward the little island with its lamp-post citadel where the officer was intrenched. I told him that we wished to enter the City by way of the Strand, whereupon he pointed out a 'bus with plenty of room on its upper deck. Then he held up that potent forefinger again, and the traffic stopped instantly while the Comédienne and I passed on in safety to the 'bus, whose driver seemed to understand through some occult means of communication with the policeman that we were fragile and to be handled with care.

To me there is something peculiarly fascinating about the top of a London 'bus. This lofty perch affords a splendid view of the street and the shops. There is an exhilarating spice of danger as the horses start off on their astonishingly swift trot considering the crowded condition of the thoroughfare; but the street is so

well paved and the swaying of the top-heavy
vehicle so gentle that one's confidence is soon
won; so that, if the weather is fine, the ride is
more enjoyable than any offered by any other
public conveyance that I know of. Even in
case of rain the waterproof lap robes with
which the seats are provided make an umbrella
the only other protection necessary. I've made
a note of these lap robes for presentation to
certain persons in America who pretend to look
after the convenience of their traveling public.
My first experience of them filled me with admiration for a nation which compels wealthy
corporations to consider the comfort of even its
humblest patrons.

"Look, look!" said the Comédienne, suddenly, when we had climbed the slender spiral
stairway to our seat on top of the 'bus. "Sairy
Gamp, as I'm alive!"

Though the horses had not yet started, the
vehicle had begun to toss like a ship in a
storm. I glanced back and saw an enormously
fat old woman stuck fast between the rails of
the stair. Her efforts to extricate herself
threatened to overturn the 'bus.

"You're too 'eavy, mum," said the conductor,
politely; "hinside's safer, mum."

"Stoopid!" said the fat lady, violently, and poked the conductor revengefully with her umbrella.

Upon this the polite conductor proceeded to boost the gigantic and tremulous bulk up the stair, while a butcher's boy on his tricycle delivery cart stopped to enjoy the spectacle.

"Hi, conductor," yelled the boy, "w'y don't yer carve off 'er corners a bit?"

A crowd began to gather and make similar comments, to all of which the fat lady turned a deaf ear. Presently, after much puffing on the part of the conductor, and an infinite number of grunts from the old woman, while it appeared that only a miracle could keep the 'bus level on its wheels, the impossible was achieved. Secure in her seat, which she overflowed into the aisle, the fat lady gasped several times, coughed asthmatically, glared at the conductor and said:

"Elephant."

"Werry appropriate," yelled the butcher's boy.

Even the polite conductor smiled discreetly behind his hand.

"Elephant, stoopid," repeated the fat lady, with another glare at the conductor.

It was irresistibly funny. The Comédienne was convulsed. The tears ran down my cheeks. The butcher's boy got off his seat and danced a joyful jig on the sidewalk.

" Elephant and Castle, dark green 'bus, mum," said the conductor.

"Stoopid!" said the old woman, her face growing crimson, as she extricated herself from her seat and lurched down the narrow stair, while the 'bus seemed in imminent danger of turning a backward summersault.

As we finally started down the Strand the fat lady was taking satisfaction out of the unwary butcher's boy with her umbrella.

The recollection of this little incident reminds me that it is the stranger in London's own fault if she ever suffers from the blues. The streets of the City present a never-ceasing spectacle of laughter-inspiring sights and sounds. These dear old Britons are so funny, and all the funnier because they are so solemnly unconscious of the fact. They say that Dickens would not know the London of to-day. Yet not five minutes after our encounter with Sairy Gamp, before we had reached the site of Temple Bar and the entrance to the City proper, we saw the Artful Dodger absorbed in the glittering display of a jeweler's window, and wondered if he had developed from his passion for "wipes" into an unholy desire for diamonds and gold chains. He was in all his details the same old Dodger—trousers much too long for him, coat sleeves turned up at the wrists and its tails dragging at his heels. Even while we gazed on him from the top of the 'bus the suspicious shopkeeper came to the door and waved him sternly away.

And, oh, the tyranny of the top hat! How that emblem of gentle leisure in America is abused in England! Fancy a baggy-kneed, manifestly poverty-stricken lawyer's clerk knocking about the courts in New York always, rain or shine, in a frowsy silk hat and a shiny frock coat. The London streets are full of just such spectacles. And such shabby coats and trousers, such abominably dilapidated, fuzzy old hats! It seems the height of absurdity that in a city where smart showers fall almost daily—when there is not a steady drizzle—the shiny beaver, whose polished surface is susceptible to the slightest moisture, should be put to such a common use. In Piccadilly you may see a Duke in a hat which would be scorned by a New York mechanic going out for

a walk in the park on Sunday afternoon. Yet,
no matter how bad the hat, how shocking the
trousers, or how disreputable the coat—even if
the coat be only a sack—their wearer is properly attired to meet gentlemen in their offices
or at their clubs on a footing of equality. Thus
attired he will receive the beautiful, smiling
courtesy so characteristic of all Englishmen in
their dealings with their equals. But let him
deny the authority of the top hat at his peril!

It seemed strange as we rumbled down the
Strand that all these centuries of traffic, and
this sea of shocking bad top hats beating
against the walls of St. Mary's had not swept
her from her foundation. There she stood like
the ice buttress of the centre pier of a Missis-
sippi river bridge dividing the torrent into two
streams, the smaller flowing through Holywell
Street on the North, to be reunited at the
Eastern end of this ecclesiastical island in
Fleet Street. Here Dr. Johnson used to bow
his obstinate old head on Sundays. Perhaps
that is the reason why the surf of traffic and
top hats continues to respect the sacred obstruc-
tion of the busiest thoroughfare in the world.

On past the Temple, catching a glimpse
through an arched way of the Temple Gardens

where the white and the red roses were plucked
for badges of loyalty to the royal houses of
Lancaster and of York, whose rival wearers
later mingled their blood on the fields of the
Wars of the Roses; past the stone Griffin
which guards the site of old Temple Bar and
the entrance to the ancient City of London,
domain of the Lord Mayor and the Guilds to
this day; down Ludgate Hill to St. Paul's;
past St. Paul's Churchyard, so calm and rest-
ful there in the very heart of the world's com-
merce, a green and soothing sanctuary; through
Cannon and West Cannon Streets, North by
King William Street into Lombard, and down
the narrow spiral stair to the pavement in front
of the Bank of England, with the Mansion
House across the way.

"Behold," said I, "the seat of government
of my new possessions."

CHAPTER V

"ALL very fine and snug and comfortable," said the Comédienne. "And I suppose that here in this solid and highly respectable institution is where you keep your surplus funds?"

"If you hadn't disturbed my lovely dream this morning," I replied, "by this time I would doubtless have moved into the Mansion House and had my hands in the cash drawer of the Bank of England. It is your own fault that we are not dividing the spoils at the present moment."

"My goodness, look what a stream of 'buses. What street can that be, dear?" The Comédienne indicated the thoroughfare leading toward the descending sun.

"That is Cheapside. A little farther on it becomes Newgate Street, then Holborn and High Holborn, and New Oxford and Oxford Street, where it enters Hyde Park. It is the great plebeian highway from the West End to

57

the East Side. Therefore the double lines of 'buses.

"That's Baedeker again. I thought I recognized the style. But, speaking of Cheapside, that reminds me. There are costermongers in Cheapside. My dear, do let's walk up that way. I yearn to behold a genuine coster on his native heath. I don't believe in the stage variety. They say their profanity is something unique and horrible. I have a depraved desire to hear some original swearing. Perhaps we can manage to have one run over by a 'bus."

So we strolled up Cheapside keeping a sharp lookout for profane costermongers.

Meanwhile a fortunate chance threw in our way an exceptionally fine illustration of the fundamental principle underlying John Bull's moral structure, which causes him to be what he is—the most uniformly successful and progressive member of the family of nations, Uncle Sam alone excepted.

The Comédienne and I had stopped in front of a chop house to gaze with watering lips at some meat pies—great fat fellows with rich brown crusts—just taken from the oven; another British institution which I respect and cherish with all my heart. There was an open coal hole in front of the shop; but as such things are not so rare in New York as to occasion comment, I merely glanced into its dark depths and passed on to the window and the meat pies. As we stepped up to the window I saw the reflection of a stubby, pompous, choleric-appearing Briton in a white waistcoat, a sack coat and a high hat, approaching from the opposite direction. Presently I saw the reflection stop on the brink of the coal hole, and heard it making indistinct objurgations. I turned and saw him walking about the hole and poking his gold-mounted stick into it. Every instant he seemed to be getting redder in the face, and after a moment I heard him exclaiming, as though to himself:

"An outrage! An imposition on the public. I'll have it stopped. Dam'me, I'll have the impudent fellow up for it!"

Whereupon the old fellow ran to the door of the shop, pounded on it loudly with his stick, calling out in a loud voice:

"Shopkeeper! I say, shopkeeper! Dam'me, I say shopkeeper! Come out here this instant, sir!"

The proprietor came to the door, rubbing his hands, but looking worried.

"Yes, sir. Certainly, sir. What can I do for you to-day, sir?"

"Dam'me, sir, you can answer a civil question. Do you see that coal hole? I say, shopkeeper, do you see that coal hole? That yawning, open coal hole? Do you see it? Do you see it? Do you see it? Dam'me, I say, do you see the coal hole?"

The shopkeeper turned pale. "Has anybody"—

"Has anybody fallen in?" repeated the old gentleman with a withering glance at the trembling proprietor. "Dam'me, a nice question for a decent, law-abiding shopkeeper to ask." Then, addressing two other gentlemen and a small boy who had stopped before the open coal hole with varying degrees of indignation expressed on their features: "He keeps open coal holes in front of his shop, dam'me, and has the presumption, the sublime insolence, to inquire whether anybody has fallen in!"

"Hi! Orficer!" yelled the small boy to a policeman passing on the other side of the street. The policeman sauntered across to the scene of the disaster, followed by half a score of plain citizens from different directions. "Orficer! I say, Orficer!"

"Move on," said the policeman.

"Orficer," explained the small boy, with horror painted on his soiled countenance, "a man has fallen into the open coal hole!"

From an elderly gentleman with a wart on his chin: "A woman has fallen into the open coal hole!"

From a youth with budding chin whiskers: "A boy has fallen into the open coal hole!"

From a rival shopkeeper next door, looking at the quaking offender as much as to say, "I always suspected it of him": "A mother and 'er young hinfant have fallen into the open coal hole!"

The policeman went on hearing further reports of the disaster until it became a wonder that any coal hole could possibly be deep enough to swallow up so large a proportion of the population.

"'E orter be chucked inter 'is own coal hole," said a cabman, strolling up with his whip in his hand.

"Oh, gentleman, I do assure you," said the shopkeeper, "it was entirely unintentional, quite, I do assure you. The coal hole was broken—I mean the lid of the coal hole, and "—

"He is actually trying to excuse his crime,

dam'me," said the choleric gentleman in the white waistcoat, with slow emphasis. " Dam'me, he actually has the impudence to make excuses ! "

" 'Ave 'im up for it ! Chuck him in ! " cried several voices.

" Move on," said the policeman, " all except the gent w'ot saw the accident."

" There was no accident," said the gentleman in the white waistcoat, with a glare at the shopkeeper, as though the fact that nobody had fallen into the coal hole was the climax of the outrage heaped on the public.

" Nobody has fallen into the coal hole," said several voices in a chorus, while the black looks that accompanied the voices seemed to indicate that the crowd would take great pleasure in tearing the miserable shopkeeper limb from limb.

" But," said the choleric gentleman, becoming purple in the face with indignation, " but I MIGHT have fallen into the coal hole, dam'me ! "

Now the full enormity of the shopkeeper's crime appeared to dawn upon the crowd.

" The gentleman MIGHT have fallen into the coal hole. Send the willain up for it," yelled the small boy.

"The gent MIGHT have fallen into the coal hole," said the cabman, indignantly.

"Yes, Officer," said the youth with budding chin whiskers, eagerly, "the gentleman MIGHT have fallen into the coal hole."

"Shopkeeper," said the policeman, sternly, "this gent MIGHT ha' fallen into the coal hole!"

I began to tremble for the poor shopkeeper. Fortunately at this juncture a man with soot on his face came up with the lid of the coal hole, carefully mended, which he put in place. Instantly the crowd moved on as though nothing unusual had happened. The relieved shopkeeper returned to his duties, and the old gentleman in the white waistcoat, now most amiable and contented of aspect, glanced in our direction with a smile of satisfaction.

"Well, this beats anything I ever heard of," said the Comédienne, who had nearly burst with laughter at the absurdity of the scene. "Just you wait a bit; I'm going to have it out with that old gentleman."

He seemed to know what was in our minds, for he came up to the window, hat in hand, and said:

"You are strangers, Americans, I see. Can I be of any service to you?"

"Yes, thank you," said the Comédienne, as I thought ruefully of the futility of my white cotton stockings. "You can tell us, if you will, why so many busy people will waste so much time over a coal hole which has been left open for five minutes. I should judge that your own time, now"—

"My own time, madam—if you will pardon the interruption—is worth a pound a minute—yes, a guinea a minute."

"Then you are quite ten guineas out of pocket through this small affair of a coal hole—not to speak of the valuable time you are squandering on a couple of inquisitive Americans. But since you are so reckless with your money won't you please interpret the parable of the coal hole for us?"

This speech seemed to please and amuse the old gentleman not a little. He smiled at us through his spectacles and asked:

"Did you ever hear the story of the Devonshire Frogs and the Can of Milk?"

"No," replied the Comédienne; "but it sounds interesting—so far."

"It has the additional merit of being short; so I will tell it.

"Once upon a time two Frogs lived in a

spring which overflowed in a stream that ran
under arches in the foundations of a Devonshire
dairy-house. One of the Frogs was old, fat and
indolent; the other was young, energetic and
very inquisitive.

" One night while the Dairy-man was sleep-
ing the two Frogs hopped under one of the
stone arches and found themselves in the dairy-
house. Some narrow-mouthed milk cans were
cooling in the shallow stream. The inquisitive
Young Frog wondered what they were. The
Old Frog advised him not to be too curious. But
the inquiring mind of the Young Frog was filled
with a yearning for wisdom that would not be
denied. So, finding a can that lay partly on its
side, he jumped in through its narrow mouth.

" After a moment of silence the curiosity of
the Old Frog, too, became excited, and he hopped
up to the mouth of the can.

" ' What are you doing in there? ' he croaked
to his young companion.

" ' Enjoying myself,' croaked back the Young
Frog. ' Hop in. It's nice and dry in here—
just the place for your rheumatism.'

" Hearing this the Old Frog gave a mighty
hop and landed on top of the Young Frog at the
bottom of the can.

" But while the two Frogs were taking a comfortable nap in the bottom of the can the industrious Dairy-man entered with the dawn and began filling the cans with milk. Soon the inquisitive Frogs were awakened by a drenching shower of some unfamiliar liquid which fell upon them, half filling the can.

"'Oh, I don't like this,' croaked the Young Frog. 'I don't like the taste of it. I'm going to leave.'

"'It's milk,' croaked the Old Frog. 'I fell into some once before. It ain't good for a Frog's health.'

" And the two Frogs began swimming about in the can and trying to climb up its smooth sides. After a little they felt the can being lifted up, and then set down hard. And presently there was steady jolting that made it still more impossible for them to climb up the sides of the can.

"'Oh, I can't stand this,' said the Young Frog, splashing about angrily with his awkward forelegs, and kicking out spitefully with his hind ones. 'It's an outrage on the entire Frog family.'

"'This milk is unhealthy,' said the Old Frog, coming to the surface for a breath of air. 'But

we will come to the market after a while, and
when they empty the milk we will make our
escape.' And he sank back resignedly to the
bottom of the can.

" But the indignant Young Frog kept splashing and kicking about and trying to climb out.
It was impossible for him to make an inch of
headway, but he kept on trying, continually
saying angrily, as he splashed and kicked:

"' Oh, I can't stand this. I won't stand it.
It's an outrage. It must be looked into. The
guilty parties shall not escape. They shall
suffer dearly for it!'

"And thus the Young Frog went on kicking
and splashing and expostulating angrily until
the Dairy-man reached the market.

"When the Dairy-man looked into the can
where the Frogs were he uttered an exclamation
of astonishment, upon which several persons
who were standing near came and looked into
the can also. And this is what they saw:

"The indolent, fat Old Frog, all puffed up,
and ghastly, lay on his back, stone dead; but
the energetic Young Frog, in perfect health and
spirits, sat comfortably on a little floating island
of butter which his constant splashing and
kicking had churned."

"Thank you, sir," said the Comédienne, hastily; "you needn't mind about the moral. I understand perfectly, now. It is their appreciation of the prime importance of kicking that has made Englishmen what they are."

The old gentleman, beaming amiably through his spectacles, waved us a pleasant farewell, and we resumed our stroll up Cheapside.

"Now if we can only find a real profane costermonger," said the Comédienne, "I, for my part, shall begin to consider myself an authority on the Peculiarities of the Englishman at Home. Aren't they funny, dear."

Now Leadenhall Market is not far from the beginning of Cheapside, though we were then unaware of the fact. But it was a fact that enabled our special ambition to be readily realized. We had not proceeded far from the scene of the coal hole incident when, from one of the narrow side streets there emerged a small, two-wheeled cart surmounted by a very large, round-faced man, about whom were heaped a choice assortment of vegetables. We instantly recognized the man's "make-up." The Comédienne clapped her hands, crying:

"There he is! I take back all I said about the stage coster. I apologize to Dan Leno and

Chevalier. But, bless my soul, are the London costers so progressive as to have electric carts?"

The cart with its load was moving rapidly along, darting this way and that to avoid collision with 'buses, without any apparent means of locomotion. To increase the mystery the round-faced man was vigorously poking down at something in front of the cart, which he was apostrophizing after this fashion:

"Now then, Jumbo! Hi s'y, Jumbo! W'ot are yer a-thinkin' of? Take a wheel hoff the bloomink 'bus, would yer? Blast yer bleedin' hears! Oh, Hi s'y, yer would, would yer? Move on, Jumbo. This ain't no bloomink bank 'oliday. Oh, wot a sassy hass it is! W'ot a sassy, disrespectful hass, an' 'e 'avin' fresh cowcumbers for 'is supper hevery night! Now Hi s'y, Jumbo!"

A sudden turn of the cart to escape a 'bus coming from the opposite direction gave us a momentary glimpse of "Jumbo"—the smallest donkey I ever saw. It seemed a miracle that he could move the heavily loaded cart. The round-faced man could have picked him up and carried him under his arm. The little beast's dexterity in escaping collisions with 'buses was marvelous.

"Hurry up, dear," said the Comédienne. "He can never get past the next corner. Look at the crush of vehicles."

So, half running, we followed the cart, feeling that the opportunity was one of a lifetime. And we were not disappointed—at least in one part of the programme. In trying to dodge between a 'bus and a cab moving rapidly in different directions the donkey lost his grip on the smooth pavement. In an instant the air was full of fresh vegetables, which descended in a shower upon the head of the big coster, seated with legs wide apart in the middle of the street, while the donkey, unhurt, though the cart was wrecked, lunched composedly off a turnip.

"Hush!" whispered the Comédienne, excitedly. "It's coming. Don't lose a word!"

The big coster's face was purple. His chest heaved. He clutched at his throat, opening and closing his mouth mechanically. At length he choked once or twice and said, slowly and distinctly:

"Well! They ain't—not—no—words!"

The Comédienne and I took the first 'bus back to our hotel.

CHAPTER VI

THE GINGPOOR OF KERHOOT

I HAVE been advised to omit all reference to the Gingpoor of Kerhoot. Certain envious members of my profession being under suspicion of having circulated the current grossly exaggerated and malicious reports of the incident in which that person figured, my well-meaning advisors argue that a discreet and dignified silence on my part would be the most effective manner of disposing of the matter. But I cannot agree with them. The Gingpoor of Kerhoot is still a favorite topic for discussion at the clubs and at afternoon teas at the best houses. He is only discussed in connection with the occurrence of which I was the innocent victim. That occurrence is the only one which can be construed as dimming by the smallest possible cloud the brilliancy of my social success in London. What, then, would be the logical inference if I should describe in detail all the numerous honors heaped upon me and pass over in silence the Gingpoor of Kerhoot? Would not the publication of these memoirs, thus incomplete, be the signal for a revival of that calumny? Who could I expect to accept as the simple truth the circumstantial accounts of my meeting with the Prince of Wales; of the distinguished attentions of Lord Dangerford; of the amiability of the Duchess of Edgecombe; of the highly flattering rivalry of Countess Pipedreme; and of my influence on diplomatic relations between the two countries—as openly admitted by the Marquis of Silsbury—who, I repeat, could be expected to accept in the proper spirit these complimentary revelations if I should commit the error of overlooking the Gingpoor of Kerhoot? No. Silence might be dignified; but, clearly, it would not be wise.

Strangely enough, I am indebted to one of my well-meaning countrymen for this solitary embarrassing detail of my career in the British capital. I owe the Gingpoor of Kerhoot to Mr. Algernon Cuff, the wealthy Broadway haberdasher. Mr. Cuff is a small, pale gentleman with thin hair. But what he lacks in size, color, and natural covering for his scalp, he more than makes up in perseverance. I am compelled reluctantly to admit that this same quality which has won such fame for his neckties and his pajamas Mr. Cuff has applied to his ambitious with respect to the writer of these memoirs. There may have been a time, before my art had secured me the independence I now enjoy, when Mr. Cuff might have—but no matter. Let us come to the Gingpoor of Kerhoot.

One night after the performance as I was changing from stage to street costume, Prue, my maid, brought me a note. I at once recognized the handwriting.

"Prue," I said, much annoyed, "this is the sixth note Mr. Cuff has sent to my dressing-room this week."

"The seventh," said Prue; "he sent in two during the matinee."

"Very well, Prue; from Mr. Cuff that is seven too many. Tell him I am very tired and shall go directly home, according to my unvarying custom."

Prue having left my dressing-room door ajar my annoyance was increased by the discovery that Mr. Cuff had evidently made an ally of Jack, our stage door guardian. He was on the stage. I could hear his high-pitched, thin voice arguing with Prue. He was pushing his way to my very door. Soon he was addressing me through the crack:

" Ah, there, Miss Casino. Peek-a-boo!"

"Really, Mr. Cuff," I said, " this is "—

" The opportunity of a lifetime," broke in the haberdasher, talking rapidly. "I am here to conduct you into the presence of His Royal Highness the Gingpoor of Kerhoot."

" The—who?" I asked in astonishment, putting on my hat as I left my dressing-room.

" The Gingpoor of Kerhoot. A most distinguished honor, I assure you."

"And who may the Gingpoor of Kerhoot happen to be, Mr. Cuff?"

The haberdasher smiled upon me with an air of superiority as he replied:.

" One of the native princes of India, lately arrived on his first visit to London. Fabulously wealthy and extremely exclusive."

" Extremely exclusive," I repeated, looking Mr. Cuff calmly in the eyes; "will you be good enough to inform me how you happen to be so chummy with His Royal Highness?"

" Well, I—er—I "— began the haberdasher, flushing, and then going on rapidly, "you see I had the good fortune to render the Prince a slight service—recently."

"Where am I invited to meet the Gingpoor of Kerhoot, Mr. Cuff?"

"At his apartments in the Tower of Babel."

"The Tower of Babel?" I repeated, surprised. As every one knows, the Tower of Babel is probably the largest and most celebrated hotel in the world. But it did not seem to me an appropriate place for a native prince of India to establish himself with his numerous retinue. I said so to Mr. Cuff, who seemed embarrassed for a moment, and then replied with his customary glibness:

"I forgot to mention that the Prince is traveling incog, accompanied by only two or three trusted servants. He is known at the hotel simply as Mr. Chunder, of Bombay."

I thought a moment, and then said:

"Surely, Mr. Cuff, you can't expect me to accept an invitation to visit the Gingpoor of Kerhoot in his apartments at midnight without knowing what sort of people I shall meet there?"

"Certainly not," replied the haberdasher, easily. "Besides several artists and literary people, there will be present Countess Pipedreme, Lord Dangerford"—

"I am quite satisfied, Mr. Cuff. Of course I shall go chaperoned."

At this remark Mr. Cuff's face seemed to become several inches longer.

"Certainly, chaperones are often indispensable," he said, giving me a tender glance; "but, in view of our long acquaintance I hoped"—

"Then you should have fixed your hopes on a different object, Mr. Cuff," I said, giving the little man a glance of severity. "I visit the Gingpoor of Kerhoot accompanied by my chaperon, or not at all."

Mr. Cuff had the good sense to concede the point instantly, and the Comédienne making her appearance at that moment dressed for the street, the three of us entered Mr. Cuff's carriage and were whirled rapidly to the Tower of Babel.

I forgot to mention Mr. Cuff's statement that as the affair was entirely informal it was unnecessary for us to dress for the occasion. So it was only a few minutes past midnight when we were ushered into the august presence of the Gingpoor of Kerhoot.

My readers do not need to be informed that the prejudice against persons of color, so universal in America, does not exist in London. That the African and his American or European descendants cut no figure in London so-

ciety is accounted for by the fact that their civilization has been so recently accomplished that
the savage still shines through their dark skin.
It is a question of intelligence, culture, refinement; not of color. Accordingly, the high
caste Indian with his centuries of intellectual
refinement, is received on terms of equality in
the best circles, though his color may be nearly,
if not quite, as dark as that of his benighted
African brother.

My first glance at the Gingpoor of Kerhoot
was reassuring. His color was satisfactory; so
were his features, which were regular; so was
his costume, which was that of a native Indian
of the highest caste. He took my hand, when
I had been presented by Mr. Cuff, and said in
very good English:

"The honor is mine. During the three days
that I have spent in England your name has
been more frequently in my ears than any other."

Then the Gingpoor of Kerhoot waved a
slender hand and two dark-skinned attendants
began serving tea.

"Oh, Miss Casino," said a sugary voice at my
elbow. "I have so longed to meet you."

"Countess Pipedreme," said little Mr. Cuff,
pompously.

This was my first actual meeting with a member of the nobility. I found the Countess at first very gracious. She was a slight, blue-eyed doll of a creature. After a moment I found that there was something disturbing in her expression, as she fixed those blue eyes, so wide open, upon me. I couldn't imagine what it was. While I was puzzling over this, a tall, boyish-appearing gentleman approached us. The Countess shrugged her shoulders slightly, and then said, in a hard, clear voice:

"Miss Casino, my dearest friend, Lord Dangerford. We were school children together."

I glanced at the enameled cheeks of Countess Pipedreme, then at the fresh, youthful countenance of Lord Dangerford, and thought how backward in her studies the Countess must have been if what she said were true—that they had been school children together. So this was the mighty hunter of big game who had complimented me so engagingly in his notes sent to my dressing-room on the opening night. He had an honest, frank countenance, with a slight diffidence which I immediately set down to his long absences from the civilized world. I liked him from the first, for I felt that he was a man of honor.

As Lord Dangerford, flushing slightly, indicated a couple of unoccupied chairs in a somewhat secluded part of the room—now rapidly filling with literary and artistic personages of both sexes—and we moved carelessly in that direction, I noticed that the Countess shrugged her shoulders again, a gesture that was almost imperceptible, yet to me as eloquent as words.

Before we had reached the vacant chairs we were overtaken by Mr. Cuff, who said, with the air of a master of ceremonies:

"Now, Miss Casino, I shall be pleased to present you to "—

"Oh, bother," said Lord Dangerford, amiably. "Never mind the literary chaps. They're probably hungry, anyway."

"But—but, think of your professional interests," began the disappointed little haberdasher, when I broke in cuttingly:

"Mr. Cuff, oblige me by not talking shop."

Whereat the haberdasher, casting upon me a reproachful look, began the difficult task of making himself agreeable to the other guests.

"This little gentleman, this Mr.—Cuff?—have you known him long?" inquired His Lordship, as we seated ourselves.

"He is an American acquaintance of some

years' standing," I replied indifferently. "I had not seen him for a long time; but when one is in a foreign country, you understand?"—

"I understand," said Lord Dangerford, with his gentle smile; "compatriots in a foreign country ignore class distinctions. One would hardly imagine, now, that this Mr.—Cuff—belonged to the diplomatic service."

"Little Mr. Cuff in the diplomatic service!" I laughed. "Why Mr. Cuff sells shirts, and—pajamas."

"Dear me," murmured His Lordship with an expression of gentle horror. "A tradesman? Dear me, dear me."

"Lord Dangerford," I said, with a feeling of rising indignation against the little haberdasher, "is your presence here the result of false representations on the part of Mr. Cuff?"

"How could that be, Miss Casino, when I find you here?"

I smiled my acknowledgments of the delicate compliment, but had the presence of mind to restrain my desire to repay it in kind.

"I think it was the Countess," explained His Lordship, "who mentioned that Mr.—Cuff,—in presenting the Gingpoor of Kerhoot's invitation, volunteered the information that he was attached to the American legation."

"The only possible connection Mr. Cuff could have with our diplomatic service," I said indignantly, "is the chance that he may have measured some of the minor attachés for new outfits of pajamas."

"Dear me, dear me," murmured His Lordship.

"Lord Dangerford," I said, suddenly, a startling suspicion having entered my mind, "have you ever traveled in India?"

His Lordship smiled. "I have killed every species of big game that country produces, including the white cow with the sacred hump on her back—for which crime, I may remark, I was arrested at the command of the Mararajah of Serat, and narrowly escaped with my life."

"Then you must have met, or at least heard of, the Gingpoor of Kerhoot?" I said, eagerly.

Lord Dangerford shook his head slowly.

"I believe the Gingpoor of Kerhoot is an impostor," I said, hotly. "I don't believe he is even 'Mr. Chunder of Bombay.'"

"I know all the Chunders of Bombay," said His Lordship, rising languidly. "This is not one of them. Pardon me, Miss Casino, if I leave you for a single moment. I'm going to address the Gingpoor of Kerhoot in his native tongue."

The instant Lord Dangerford had left his chair Mr. Cuff slid into it. He seemed much excited.

"Miss Casino," he began, speaking rapidly and twisting the fingers of one hand with the fingers of the other in a most nervous and disturbing manner, "Miss Casino, you must understand why I brought you here."

"Certainly I do," I replied. "It was to meet the Gingpoor of Kerhoot."

"Oh, d——n the Gingpoor of Kerhoot—er—excuse the feelings of a desperate man. Miss Casino, can you look upon me and not be aware that I adore you?"

"Mr. Cuff," said I, "your adoration is very flattering, but if you imagine that gratitude for the means of meeting the Gingpoor of Kerhoot will change the sentiments I have always felt toward you"—

"The Gingpoor of Kerhoot be—hanged," said the miserable little haberdasher, making an awkward attempt to take possession of one of my hands. "Can't you, oh, won't you, realize that it was all for the opportunity of opening my heart to you that I arranged this"—

"Then you admit, Mr. Cuff, that the Gingpoor of Kerhoot is an impostor?" And I rose from my chair with a gesture of disgust which seemed to wring the haberdasher's very soul.

"Oh, no, no. Not that, I assure you, on the honor of a gentleman. Not that. Oh, no, no, no!" The little man had a fold of my skirt in his hand, and was almost groveling at my feet.

"Mr. Cuff," said I, "you are making a spectacle of yourself. Why, what is the meaning of this?"

Something was occurring that brought even the haberdasher to his senses. The Gingpoor of Kerhoot and Lord Dangerford were surrounded by a dozen whispering guests who were casting scornful looks at the dark-skinned potentate. The changed aspect of this personage was startling. His lips, once so red, were now ashen, and his eyes rolled in terror. In a cool, stern voice Lord Dangerford was addressing him in a language quite unfamiliar to my ears. Presently he ceased, as though awaiting a reply. The Gingpoor of Kerhoot opened and closed his mouth once or twice, muttered half a dozen disconnected words, evidently in the same language used by His Lordship, and then collapsed in a heap on a divan, while a majority of the guests made hurried preparations for departure.

"Why, wh—what does this mean?" stuttered the haberdasher, rubbing his eyes.

"A very pertinent question," commented Lord Dangerford, resuming his place at my side, and casting upon poor Mr. Cuff that other glance which lurked in those blue eyes which, up to this moment, I had found so mild. It occurred to me that this was the look with which His Lordship brought down his big game.

"Why,—why, everybody is going!" exclaimed innocent Mr. Cuff in dismay. "It isn't late—for London."

"Lord Dangerford," said Countess Pipedreme, coming up with her wraps on, "I am ready." Her wrap barely brushed the sleeve of Mr. Cuff's coat; but she drew it away with a gesture that caused the blood to mount to the haberdasher's cheeks.

"I—I don't understand," began the trembling master of ceremonies; "I"—

"Where did you pick up the—Gingpoor of Kerhoot?" demanded His Lordship.

"He sent his servant to my apartment," the haberdasher explained, eagerly. "The servant said that the Prince, for diplomatic reasons, did not wish to make himself known in London. He was traveling incog with only three attendants. One of the servants, taking advantage of the Prince's desire to conceal his rank, had stolen all his jewels and ready money, amounting to nearly a million rupees. The servant said that the Prince had of course immediately communicated with the royal treasury in India, but in the meantime he was entirely without means. I called on the Prince, and found that the honest servant had told the exact truth.

"Of course," added the haberdasher, modestly, "I was happy to render the Gingpoor of Kerhoot any assistance in my power."

"Of course," assented His Lordship. "How much, Mr.—Cuff—has the Gingpoor of Kerhoot cost you to date?"

"Oh!" exclaimed the little haberdasher, turning pale, "you don't mean—you surely can't mean—that the Prince is an—an"—

"An imposter, yes, that's the word, Mr.—Cuff."

"Oh!" almost screamed the miserable little man, beating his breast. "My two hundred pounds—or was it two hundred guineas?—oh, it was guineas, I'm sure it was guineas!"

At this juncture there was a welcome interruption in the person of the American Friend. While Mr. Cuff was still lamenting his ravished guineas, the American Friend quickly took in the situation. Really this wonderful man seems to know everybody. He walked up to where the Gingpoor of Kerhoot crouched in terrified silence, took him by the collar, and dragged him, all resplendent in his oriental robes, to the door of an inner room where he said:

"George Washington Johnson, if I ever catch you at any more of your tricks I'll live to see you hanged!"

And with that the American Friend gave the late Gingpoor of Kerhoot a mighty kick which sent him sprawling through the door.

Then the American Friend explained that George Washington Johnson had been the colored valet of a certain well-known promoter whose business had at one time taken him to Bombay.

When he was assured that the American Friend would accompany me to my hotel, Lord Dangerford said some friendly words of farewell and departed with the Countess. We left Mr. Cuff beating his breast and moaning:

"Oh, my two hundred pounds! Or was it guineas? I am almost sure it was guineas."

CHAPTER VII

TWO FLAGS THAT WAVE AS ONE

On a certain night, never to be forgotten, I noticed at the beginning of the second act that the audience seemed unusually sympathetic. We had grown accustomed to our success with these Londoners, many of whose faces had become familiar to us, so constant was their attendance; but on the night to which I refer there was an enthusiasm in their applause which seemed entirely disproportionate to our merits as entertainers. To be strictly accurate, I was not the first to make this discovery. I do not make my entrance until some minutes after the curtain has risen on the second act; not, in fact, until Little Bobby, Tommy Atkins, Daffy and several others have appeared in an opening scene and retired from the stage to dress for the ensemble. So it happened that it was Little Bobby, now quite an accomplished cockney, as to dialect, who brought me the news, shouting as she pitched headlong into my dressing-room:

"Hooray! We've regerlarly fetched 'em at larst."

I applied a touch of carmine to the centre of my upper lip—the touch that gives me my "prunes and prisms" expression.

"Bless their bloomink 'earts, just 'ear 'em!" And Little Bobby turned a delighted ear toward my open door.

Sure enough. For the first time since our opening sounds of applause reached my dressing room. I gave Little Bobby a glance of inquiry, and went on experimenting with my "prunes and prisms" effect. Instead of answering, Little Bobby opened the door to its full width and held up a finger invoking attention.

My dressing-room being close to the proscenium on the "O. P." side of the stage I could hear quite distinctly the bursts of applause that were coming from the audience, mingled with half articulate murmurs of admiration. Presently there was a louder burst than usual, above which we heard distinctly in a shrill voice coming apparently from the gallery:

"Hooray for Uncle Sam! God save the Queen!"

"Little Bobby," said I, "coming from a British audience this is marvelous." And I hastily finished preparations for my entrance.

"It's 'igh time they 'oorayed for Uncle Sam; but w'ot are they ringing the Queen into it for?"

"Hush!" said I. "Patriotism begins at home. It is marvelous that we should be the means of having America cheered at all. Something has happened that we are not yet aware of."

"Your scene, Miss Casino," warned the call boy.

Hurrying to respond to my cue, I was greeted by a storm of hand-clapping that for a moment completely bewildered me. I was shocked back into lucidity by that same shrill voice in the gallery repeating:

"Hooray for Uncle Sam! God save the Queen!"

Even the distinguished-looking occupants of the boxes were clapping their gloved hands and laughing good-humoredly.

The applause continued at intervals throughout the act, and when, just before the fall of the curtain, our squad of United States marines entered and marched to their position at the centre of the stage, and from opposite wings the Stars and Stripes and the Union Jack were brought in and borne side by side above the heads of the marines—a detail which had not been omitted at any previous performance—half the great audience rose and cheered lustily, while the orchestra played The Star Spangled Banner.

What had happened? The moment the curtain had fallen we were asking this question of each other. Several of the girls showed signs of hysterics. Others walked about absently, humming patriotic airs. I observed our American property man furtively brushing away a tear. My own eyes were moist. Little Bobby was sniffing audibly. Oh, it was very plain that our London success had not hardened our hearts. We were still Americans!

As we stood in an agitated group speculating and wondering, I heard the voice of the American Friend addressing me.

"Miss Casino, you've met Lord Dangerford. He comes to tell you the news—good news. Glorious news!"

His Lordship was smiling. "Miss Casino, how do you like England to-night?"

" Meat pies and Duchesses."—Page 91.

"I have always liked England," I answered. " To-night I love her."

"So d—do I," said Little Bobby, wiping her eyes.

"As for me, I dote on England," said the Comédienne, who held her handkerchief in her hand, and whose nose was red. When the Comédienne is agitated she makes the most grotesque remarks. When Lord Dangerford had asked her politely what characteristic product of Great Britain she doted on most, she replied, with a hysterical gurgle:

"Meat pies and Duchesses."

"And what," said His Lordship, still smiling amiably, "do you think we Englishmen admire most about America. No joking, my dear young ladies; this is serious."

His Lordship was still smiling, but gravely, as though the thing of which he was thinking lay very close to his heart. We were silent. Lord Dangerford paused for a moment, then took off his hat and said:

"To-night we Englishmen are filled with admiration for the American navy. We would like to shake hands with every brave blue jacket that walks the decks of your battle ships. We would like to stand beside them at your guns, with gallant Commodore Dewey on the bridge of the flagship."

"The war with Spain," I asked eagerly, while all the members of the company gathered close about Lord Dangerford; "has it really begun? Has there been a great victory?"

"Almost the greatest naval victory ever won," said His Lordship. "A splendid, gallant attack by the American squadron. A magnificent dash in the early morning right under the muzzles of the great guns of the Spanish land batteries, heedless of torpedoes and sunken mines, on at full speed into the harbor of Manila where the Spanish fleet lay, five glorious hours of fighting, and then not a Spanish ship left above water."

"Oh, our poor sailors," said I; "what an awful slaughter it must have been!"

"Not an American killed; only a few wounded," said Lord Dangerford.

We looked at one another in amazement.

"The marksmanship of the American gunners was superb," said His Lordship. "By this time all Europe is singing their praises."

You should have seen us there, in our wigs, our painted faces, in the tinsel and the silken fripperies of our mimic world attire,—uncon-

scious of the incongruity of bare shoulders and
arms and shapely limbs unconventionally ex-
posed, with the great deeds being pictured to us
so graphically—alternately hugging each other,
dancing for joy, and returning eagerly to His
Lordship for more details. We were none the
less Americans for being mummers, and I am
sure that Lord Dangerford, upon that occasion,
regarded us in no other light than of representatives of a nation which he, in his impulsive
way, delighted to honor. The news of the battle, too late for publication in the London evening papers, had been received at the theatre
during the first act. By the time the curtain
rose on the second act every one in the house
knew of the disaster which the Spaniards had
suffered in their first encounter with American battle ships. There is nothing that stirs
the blood of an Englishman, to whatever class
he may belong, like war and tales of gallant
fighting. So, in default of actual heroes of
Manila to cheer, they cheered us. They kept it
up until the close of the performance. And
when I stepped into my hansom at the stage
door the narrow street was filled with late occupants of the pit and the gallery, who cheered
us as we departed for our homes.

As days passed by it was delightful to note that this new spirit of cordiality toward Americans was not merely an impulse inspired by unexpected revelations of valor in battle, to die out when the news had grown cold. Londoners of every station in life seemed to take personal and permanent pride in the new and honorable character acquired by a sister nation. It had seemed to me before the battle of Manila that Englishmen did not consider America and Americans quite seriously. If one found occasion to refer to the population, the institutions and the resources of the United States, and to show how favorably they compared with those of any other country, the most one could expect in reply would be a patronizing reference to the "opportunity" which England had permitted the fathers of the American revolution to grasp. In other words, the United States was a sort of accident, which might, or might not turn out well, according to circumstances. The fact that the victories which had won us our independence had been duplicated by others equally brilliant a quarter of a century later appeared to have no special significance to our obstinate brother. His attitude was that of an elder near relative who had made a domestic

concession out of sheer good nature. Troubles
like these were bound to occur in the best regulated families. The easiest way to smooth them
over was for the powerful elders to appear to
let the insurgent youthful member of the family
have his own way.

But now that the lusty young prodigal had
thrown down the gauntlet to a legitimate
enemy, which he had proceeded to whip in
the most gallant and scientific style known in
modern warfare, his deed not only established
his personal status, but reflected credit on the
entire family. It was therefore but the simplest logic that all English hearts should warm
toward us after our first superb dash at the
throat of the Spaniard.

As I am only an ignorant girl engrossed
wholly in the arts of peace, you will understand that my impressions, as above feebly expressed, come necessarily very near the truth.
I possess neither the knowledge nor the sophis-
try which blunts the observation of the wise
ones and so often leads them to false conclusions. A single illustration, added to that furnished by the enthusiasm of Lord Dangerford,
will be sufficient to convince the most skeptical
that great truths may issue from a frivolous

and petticoated creature of the footlights as well as from the mouths of babes and sucklings.

It was perhaps a week after we received the great news from the Philippines that I found it necessary to do some shopping in Regent and Oxford Streets.

"Prue," said I as I stepped into the hansom waiting outside the arched gateway of the pretty little place in St. John's Wood which I now inhabited; "Prue, can you think of anything besides the gloves, the hat I need for the coaching party to the Ascot Cup race, the black silk hose, and the shirt waists?"

"No," answered my maid, who is really my companion as well; "and there is really no hurry about the shirt waists. You have three that you've never worn."

At this time the Honorable Mrs. Pebblestone, of whom I shall have more to say later on, had become one of my warmest friends. Her introductions at the best shops in the fashionable district insured my being waited on with the utmost deference. But I was quite unprepared for the attentions that were showered upon me by the proprietors themselves upon this occasion. The shop where I stopped to purchase gloves is regularly patronized by the Princess of Wales. My hansom had hardly stopped before its entrance when the proprietor, bare headed, came out and escorted me into his establishment.

"It is an honor to serve you, Miss Casino, I do assure you," he said smilingly. Then, having ordered an attendant to exhibit his entire stock for my inspection, he remarked:

" What a glorious victory, that of Commodore Dewey's, at Manila."

"It's so lovely of you Englishmen to take such interest in our brave sailors," I said, with a smile of gratitude. " Thanks, I'll take these —yes, the whole half dozen. I like the style, and they seem so well stitched."

" Your Commander Dewey deserves to rank with our own Nelson," said the shopkeeper.

" Do you really think so? How delightful! I'll take half a dozen of the undressed tans, please."

" The marksmanship of your gunners is the absorbing topic of conversation in our naval circles, my son says, who is home on two months' leave."

" Why," said I in joyful surprise, " I always supposed that the English gunners had no equals. Yes, two pairs of the two-button, and two pairs of the driving gauntlets. One cannot have too many gloves, especially when they are so well made as these are."

" Wherever I go," the shopkeeper resumed, " I hear the most enthusiastic praise of the personal bravery of the Americans. Only yesterday the Prince was in to select a dozen pairs of driving gloves, and I ventured to remark to His Royal Highness that it was glorious to think that these 'eroes were of our own flesh and blood."

" What did the Prince say," I asked, eagerly.

" His Royal Highness remarked that blood was thicker than water, and he was proud of it."

" How beautiful of the Prince!" said I. " Oh, a dozen of the Suedes, please."

My reception at the other shops was no less flattering. I was amazed to note what an intimate knowledge of American affairs these London shopkeepers have. They related to me particulars of the battle of Manila which I had been unable to find in any of the newspapers. Their honest faces beamed with joy while they eulogized the genius and gallantry of Dewey, and recited instances of the personal bravery of his men. They seemed to be wholly indifferent as to whether I made any purchases. Their pride in their kinship with Americans was delightful to behold. I drove home with my purchases heaped around me in the hansom feeling as though I had a personal share in the new lustre shed upon my country.

Occasionally Prue presumes upon her not wholly admitted status as my companion. This was her disposition when I reached home.

"Forty-seven pairs of gloves!" she exclaimed. "You didn't say anything about having to purchase for all the other girls, too."

"I purchased only for myself," I replied in tones becoming to the principal in the transaction.

"Did you purchase nine hats for yourself only?" demanded Prue, taking them from their boxes.

I nodded.

"And eleven shirt waists?"

"One needs a change, occasionally," I replied, cuttingly.

"Half a dozen pink and half a dozen black silk hose, at thirteen and six a pair. One would say, my dear, that you imagined yourself a centipede."

I declined to pursue the conversation. It would have been impossible to make Prue, whose nature is cold and practical, understand the patriotic feelings which prompted me to recognize the beautiful expressions of pride and sympathy which had flowed from the hearts of these honest London shopkeepers.

CHAPTER VIII

I HAD now attained that social eminence, striven for by so many in my profession, achieved by so few, which made me the object of the attentions of a Duchess. Believe me, I do not mention this with any desire of provoking the envy of my less fortunate sisters; it is only one of those things which the veracious historian is in duty bound to record. Furthermore, I must do myself the justice of explaining that this and other distinctions came to me quite unsolicited. As the best possible evidence to that effect I will quote from the Honorable Mrs. Pebblestone's letter containing an invitation to which I was preparing to respond one lovely afternoon in June.

"My dear," wrote the Honorable Mrs. Pebblestone, "I hope you will appreciate the real significance of the compliment Her Grace bestows upon you. The Duchess of Edgecombe is not one of those extremely modernized members of the nobility who stultify themselves and their position by constant efforts to conciliate the masses. She is hardly less faithful to the tenets of the ancient regime than is the Dowager Duchess herself. Yet, my dear child, it is the Dowager Duchess who is the more urgent of the two in pressing this invitation upon you.

"So, my dear, if the Dowager Duchess, who goes out rarely, and never to the theatre—she is past eighty, you know—should ask you to sing something, you will of course understand that she makes the request in the same spirit that she would make it of the Countess Pipedreme, Lady Dunstable or of any other of the accomplished amateurs moving in our best society. . . .

" My carriage will call for you, dear, at four precisely. Do not be a moment late, I beg of you. At Edgecombe House tea is served punctually on the stroke of five—a point upon which the Dowager Duchess is extremely particular.

"Faithfully yours,
"Peggy Pebblestone."

I read the Honorable Mrs. Pebblestone's letter to Prue while she was dressing my hair.

"Ahem," said my companion-maid, as though about to make one of her critical observations, but finally concluding that silence was more discreet.

"Well, Prue?" I said interrogatively.

"Oh, I know just how much weight my opinion will have with you."

"But you don't need to pull my hair out by the roots in your efforts to suppress your natural inclination to say disagreeable things. I would rather you spoke out," said I.

"Well," said Prue, "I have only one fault to find with the Honorable Mrs. Pebblestone's letter containing the Dowager Duchess' invitation for you to sing at the Duchess of Edgecombe's afternoon tea."

"And what may that be, Prue?"

"That the Honorable Mrs. Pebblestone's letter did not also contain the Dowager Duchess' check for ten guineas."

"Prue," I replied in a tone that forbade further discussion of the subject, "the Honorable Mrs. Pebblestone's carriage is waiting at my door. When you have finished with my hair I will go."

It is so easy for some people to suspect base motives in even the friendliest actions of others.

I am proud to say that I accepted the Duchess of Edgecombe's flattering attention in the spirit which prompted it. The Honorable Mrs. Pebblestone beamed with pleasure when I arrived at her house on time; and during our short drive to Edgecombe House she overwhelmed me with compliments of what she was pleased to term my simple and unaffected manner of accepting attentions which were my due.

"It is so good of you to come, my dear," said the Duchess of Edgecombe, kissing me cordially on both cheeks. "Come, I must present you to mamma, who is dying to meet you."

The Duchess led me into a room where the tea things were already spread. At the upper end of the room behind a table evidently reserved for her exclusive use sat a very large old lady with a double chin, blinking red eyelids and innumerable iron-grey curls brushing her mottled cheeks. Before I realized who the old lady was it occurred to me how much she resembled a toad—and not a very amiable one either.

"Mamma is becoming forgetful, and a little deaf," said the Duchess, as we drew near the old lady entrenched behind her tea table. "But you won't mind, dear."

If the Dowager Duchess' ears had been somewhat dulled by time it was evident that her
red-rimmed eyes were still sufficiently sharp.

"Sally," she mumbled, querulously, as we
approached, "Sally, where's the tea?"

"It lacks five minutes to five yet, mamma,"
said the Duchess, in the low, distinct tones one
learns to use in speaking to deaf persons.

"The clocks are wrong again, drat it!" said
the old lady. Then, putting up a tortoise-
shell-rimmed glass she looked at me sharply
and said, shaking her grey curls solemnly:

"The new maid, Sally? No, she won't do.
Send her away, Sally. Too neat, too handsome. Think of the boys, Sally. We must
not put temptation in the way of the boys.
Send her away, Sally; send her away."

I felt that my cheeks were scarlet.

"No, no, mamma," said the Duchess, with
her lips close to the old lady's ear; "this is
Miss Casino."

"Oh, the dancing woman," said the dreadful
old lady, grinning at me through her glass.
"A good leg, no doubt; I should judge that
she had a very good leg, drat it! I dare say
now, my dear, that you could kick a globe off

the chandelier. Do it, drat it! Do it for a shilling."

The Dowager Duchess, mumbling to herself, seemed to be searching her pocket for a shilling. Her daughter-in-law checked her with a sharp explanation:

"No, no, mamma. Miss Casino. A very estimable young lady. The one who sings, you remember—of whom Lord Dangerford spoke so highly."

"Lord Dangerford is a sad young dog, Sally. I remember his father, drat it!" And the Dowager Duchess laughed softly at her memory. Then she glanced at me again sharply. "And so you sing, Miss? Well, well; after tea, after tea, perhaps. But I'm sure she has a good leg, Sally."

This embarrassing incident was closed temporarily by the entrance of servants with tea. One of the servants bore a large tray upon which, besides a pot which must have contained fully half a gallon of steaming amber fluid, were a dozen slices of buttered bread, a jar of marmalade and an imposing pyramid of cakes. To my surprise the entire contents of this tray were deposited upon the table at which the Dowager Duchess sat alone, whereupon the

servant coolly tucked a napkin under the old
lady's double chin and left the room.

In spite of my democratic origin and my
loyal adherence to the principles of republican-
ism I have always entertained a certain respect
for the institutions of royalty; but I will not
deny that the appetite of the Dowager Duchess
of Edgecombe, and her manner of satisfying it,
filled me with an amazement in which the sentiment of reverence for the nobility was con-
spicuously lacking.   When the dreadful old
woman drank her tea she gurgled; when she
ate her buttered bread she snored; when she
tossed assorted tea cakes into her cavernous
mouth she accompanied the feat by little grunts
and chuckles of satisfaction that were essen-
tially unaristocratic.   I gazed upon the feeding
Dowager Duchess with a horrible fascination
that was only interrupted by the consciousness
that I was being presented to Lady Dunstable
against a familiar background of Lord Dangerford and Countess Pipedreme.   The room had
filled with distinguished society people, with
here and there a petted artist or musician.
The Duchess, with a tact that was admirable,
classified the company according to its individual friendships and animosities, the group

of which I found myself a member having, it is true, one slight disadvantage in the person of Countess Pipedreme, who, if possible, was thicker as to enamel, and less discreet in her bearing toward Lord Dangerford, than upon the occasion of our former meeting.

"My dear," said Lady Dunstable—an amiable young matron with round cheeks and baby blue eyes—"my dear, you probably have met my brother, George Dashleigh. He has a cattle ranch somewhere in Texas—or is it Brazil? At any rate it is not far from New York."

The geographical information that rose to my lips died there in obedience to Lord Dangerford's smiling glance of warning.

"No, I never had that pleasure," I answered politely, then adding as I returned Lord Dangerford's amused glance: "I rarely go farther from New York than Alaska or Patagonia."

"Dear me," said Lady Dunstable; "why I visited Edinburgh before I was sixteen."

"I understand," drawled the Earl of Drippingeaves, "that there are no longer any buffalo within a day's ride of Washington. Sorry, I'm sure. Must be a dooced inconvenience for the sportsmen of Omaha."

The Duchess turned her friendly eyes upon me.

"How do you like London, my dear?"

"I am overawed by its size, its wealth and its splendid historical associations"—

"Of course you've been to the trial of poor, dear Dr. Cummings," said Lady Dunstable.

"As I have not yet had time to visit either the Tower or the Museum," I answered, "I naturally"—

"Oh, a great mistake, my dear," interrupted the Duchess with sparkling eyes. "There is nothing in London to compare in interest for a moment with the trial of Dr. Cummings."

"I wouldn't miss a session for worlds," said Countess Pipedreme.

"Nor I," said Lady Dunstable with a look of ecstasy.

"My dear," said the Duchess, "you never saw such a delicious look of agony on a human face as that with which Dr. Cummings listened to the damning evidence against him. It was most thrilling."

"Indeed it was," chirped Lady Dunstable, sipping her tea. "I haven't experienced such a genuine sensation since I listened to poor dear Lady Isabella Bellamy's sentence of transportation for life for choking her grandmother to death."

"Really, you mustn't dream of missing Dr. Cummings' trial," said the Duchess earnestly; "of course you have already missed the earlier sessions. But come around any morning while I am at breakfast and I will gladly give you the details of the case up to date. I know them by heart."

"So do I," said Lady Dunstable. "My dear, you shall go to the next session of the trial with me. I will have my carriage call for you in ample time."

"Thank you, Duchess; thank you, Lady Dunstable. It is very good of you," I said. "You will pardon my ignorance if I inquire the nature of the crime of which Dr. Cummings is accused?"

"Murder, my dear," said the Duchess. "The most delightfully cold-blooded murder in all the annals of crime."

"This Dr. Cummings," I said, faintly, "was he of good standing in his profession? Did he move"—

"My dear," said the Duchess, leaning across the tea table toward me, "Dr. Cummings was

my own family physician. He had my entire
confidence."

"And mine," said Lady Dunstable. "You
can't imagine, my dear, how interesting it is to
see one's confidential medical adviser trembling
in the murderer's dock. You should have seen
him on the day he fainted while undergoing the
torture of cross-examination."

"It was the most enjoyable afternoon I have
spent in years," said the Duchess, helping herself to more tea.

I have no idea how much longer this extraordinary scene would have lasted under ordinary
conditions. But the Dowager Duchess having
finished her half gallon of tea, her dozen slices
of buttered bread, and her pyramid of assorted
tea cakes, was now snoring unendurably with
her double chin buried in her bulbous bosom.

"Poor mamma," said the Duchess, in tones
of sympathy, but with a glance in the direction
of the disturbance that belied them; "she becomes so fatigued in the afternoon."

With this remark the Duchess went over and
shook the Dowager Duchess of Edgecombe so
soundly by her noble shoulder that she awoke
with a start and instantly fixed her red-rimmed
eyes upon me, saying haughtily:

"Well, why doesn't the woman dance? She's had her tea, hasn't she?"

I saw Lord Dangerford's face grow dark, and restrained my indignation.

"Well, why doesn't she sing then?" demanded the dreadful old lady, after the Duchess had whispered some words in her ear; "has she had her tea, or hasn't she? Drat it!"

Fortunately for me the Dowager Duchess was too sleepy to pursue the subject further, but dozed off again, muttering loud enough for every one to hear:

"But I'm sure she has a good leg—a good leg, drat it!"

Subsequent kindnesses on the part of the Duchess of Edgecombe, of Lady Dunstable, and other members of the British nobility, have served in a great measure to stifle my resentment against the Dowager Duchess, who, it is easy to see, is in her dotage, and therefore not accountable for either her words or her actions.

CHAPTER IX

MY duty as a faithful chronicler again compels me to recite matters which, personally, I would prefer should remain unrecorded. Not that they tend in any way to diminish my just claim to the honors which had fallen so thick upon me. I trust that the time will never come when any outcome of the lamentable feud between Daffy and the Liar could be equal to the accomplishment of that result. But I dislike to mention the particular occurrence I now have in mind for the reason that it seems to place in an undignified light one whom I esteem most highly. I refer to Lord Dangerford. But let me recite the details in the order in which they occurred, leaving my discriminating readers to place where they belong whatever blame and humiliation are merited or suffered.

I have already, once or twice, referred incidentally to the disquieting conduct of Daffy and the Liar: to their undisguised hatred of each other whenever fortune smiled upon our

prospects; to their brief and affecting reconcili-
ations in the seeming presence of disaster; and
to the spirit of discord which their example
provoked among the chorus.   It will have been
observed that the unequivocal success of our
London opening, and the added popularity we
soon enjoyed as compatriots of the gallant
Commodore Dewey, were not conducive to any
further suspensions of this extraordinary feud.
In one respect this was a fortunate circum-
stance.   Daffy had left behind her in New York
an exceedingly jealous husband.   I had often
been troubled by the thought of what unpleas-
ant consequences might follow his discovery,
for instance, of the tears and embraces with
which Daffy and the Liar adjusted their mutual
grievance during the dark hour preceding the
first rise of our curtain.   A month had now
elapsed since the occurrence of this indiscreet
scene.   Supposing some mischievous member
of the company—the Comédienne or Little
Bobby—had written to Daffy's husband about
it?   Either of these two might have done so
without meriting very severe rebuke.   Both
were known to be the possessors of American
husbands, of whom both stood in some awe,
and both had more than once, on the eve of

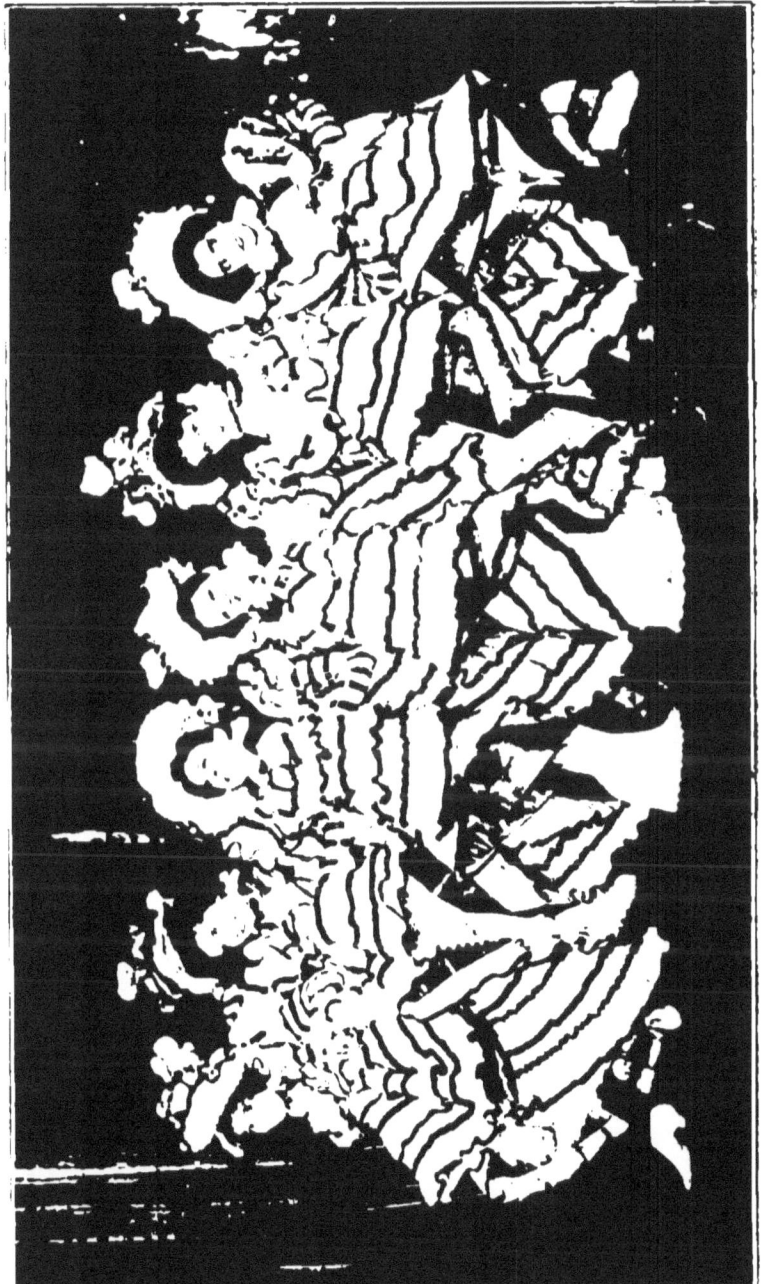

"It was near the end of the first act." —Page 115.

some merry junket up the Thames, been solemnly informed by the Liar that their husbands
had arrived some days before and were in communication with Scotland Yard.   I should have
mentioned before this that it was his frequent
indulgence in disturbing reports of this kind
that had won for the Liar his sobriquet.

On the evening of the day on which I took
tea at the Duchess of Edgecombe's my mind
was too full of other thoughts to leave room for
logical deductions regarding a disturbance behind the scenes which began during the first
act and lasted until the performance was over.
I was therefore as completely deceived as was
every other participant.

It was near the end of the first act, and the
cue for the Liar's entrance had met with no
response.   I added some impromptu lines and
then repeated the Liar's cue.   Still no response.
I glanced through the entrance where he was
due to appear and was astonished to see him
standing there ready to go on.   A second
glance showed me that something was wrong.
The Liar held an open letter in his hand at
which he was looking in a dazed fashion while
he gradually turned the color of chalk under
his make-up.   Before the audience was aware

that anything was wrong the stage manager, furious, snatched the letter from the Liar's hand and pushed him headlong upon the stage. This variation on his usual entrance was comical, and the audience laughed heartily. But there was consternation among all of us who figured in the scene. The Liar stood stupidly opening and closing his large mouth without uttering a word. I then understood that the shock of some revelation made in the letter had caused him to forget his lines.

As often happens in such cases the comedian was so much funnier thus incapacitated than when in the full enjoyment of his powers that the scene went better than ever with the audience. We pushed the Liar about the stage, making him go through the motions of his part, and managed to save the scene from absolute collapse.

The moment the curtain was down the Liar fell, gasping, into a chair.

"What is the matter?" demanded a dozen voices.

"My life has been threatened. I'm a dead man."

"What has happened? What does he say?" said Daffy, pushing her way through the circle.

"He says he's a dead man," sneered the disgusted stage manager.

In a moment Daffy was beside the frightened comedian, but he pushed her away.

"Go away, woman. You are the cause of it. My blood will be on your head. The letter. The letter. Where is the letter?"

"Here is your letter," said the stage manager, producing it; "if I ever catch you reading another during the performance I'll fine you a week's salary."

The Liar shuddered as he took the fatal document. I looked over his shoulder and read:

"Sir:

"Even the rattlesnake gives warning before he strikes his victim. Though more deadly than the rattlesnake I shall not be less magnanimous. Therefore accept this as your warning. I am here. I know all. I strike, and I strike quickly.
(Signed) "John Cutter."

"Oh, I'm a dead man," groaned the miserable object of John Cutter's approaching vengeance.

"Gee!" ejaculated Daffy, otherwise Mrs. John Cutter, turning pale, yet evincing a strong desire to comfort the Liar in his hour of trouble.

"Go away, woman," said the doomed man in agonized tones. "Even now his eyes may be upon us. Hide me, oh, hide me somewhere, can't you?"

"We'd better hide him," said Little Bobby, gravely. "There was a strange man loitering about the stage door when I came in."

"Was he tall, with a smooth shaven face?" quavered the Liar.

"Yes," said Little Bobby.

"Young looking, with blue eyes and light hair?"

"He was young looking and he had light hair," replied Little Bobby; "as to the color of his eyes, it was not light enough"—

"It is he. I'm a dead man all right. Save me, some of you. Hide me—save me!"

"We'll surely have to do something," said the Comédienne. "I know John Cutter. There's no nonsense about him, I can tell you."

The affecting scene was interrupted by the reappearance of our irrascible stage manager with peremptory orders for the Liar to get ready for the second act or hand in his resignation.

"So be it," said the doomed man, rising with a dramatic gesture. "I'm a dead man; but let it be known to all the world that I died at my post of duty."

"Die wherever you please," snarled the stage manager; "but get ready for the second act."

"I suppose I may have the privilege of telegraphing a friend to come at once and see that I have decent burial?" said the Liar.

"Send as many telegrams as you like," snapped the autocrat; "but don't let me catch you receiving any more during the performance."

We got through the second act somehow, though the audience must have realized that our minds were not on our tasks. Daffy looked half frightened to death. The Liar went through his comedy scenes as though he were playing Hamlet. Oddly enough, Little Bobby and the Comédienne whispered and giggled in the most heartless and disgraceful manner.

As I left the stage at the end of the act I found Lord Dangerford standing in the wings.

"The manager sent me around to tell you the latest war news," said His Lordship. "The first detachment of United States troops is about to sail for Cuba."

"Thank you so much," said I; "but—dear me, Lord Dangerford, what have you been doing to yourself?"

A drop of blood glistened on His Lordship's upper lip, and he was nursing his left hand as though it pained him.

"Oh, nothing. Nothing, I assure you. Merely a little altercation outside."

"An altercation? With whom? Let me look at your hand."

His Lordship objected, but I insisted. Two of his knuckles were skinned and the nail of his thumb was badly broken.

"Dear me," I said, "you must have your hand attended to, at once."

"Which is w'ot we're 'ere for, Miss, this werry hinstant," said a rough voice. And I caught the flash of something metallic thrown across the injured hand I was examining.

Before His Lordship began the astonishing evolutions which occupied the next fifteen seconds, filling the air with the sound of crushing blows and muffled curses, I saw that two short, stout men had approached him from behind while we were talking and had endeavored to

place handcuffs on his wrists. This was the
last detail of the affair that was clear to me until the evolutions of His Lordship, the sounds of
the blows and the curses seemed to be merged
into the interesting spectacle of Lord Dangerford surrounded by a ring of admiring scene-
shifters sitting on one of his assailants and
holding the other, who was all dazed and
bloody, by the collar. Two pairs of handcuffs
lay at His Lordship's feet. One of these he
placed upon the wrists of his dazed captive,
and after a brief struggle the other was treated
similarly. The men were covered with dust
and the eyes of both were beginning to turn
black. Lord Dangerford seemed to have suffered no further inconvenience.

"Will you be good enough to explain what
you mean by attacking me twice in this manner, once just before and once after my quiet
and orderly entrance here with the consent of
the manager of the theatre?" asked His Lordship, composedly.

"We're Pitchers and Duff," said one of the
men, sullenly, "from Scotland Yard, an' we're
'ere on duty."

There was a sudden movement in the crowd
of stage people which surrounded Lord Danger-

ford and his captives, and the Liar was seen pushing his way forward, screaming:

"Have you got him? Don't let him get away or I'm a dead man!"

"Are you the complainant in this 'ere case?" demanded Mr. Pitchers, with a dark look at the Liar.

"Yes, but what—where—who"—

"Well, there's your man," said Mr. Pitchers, indicating His Lordship. "Look out for 'im. 'E's a bad 'un, ain't 'e, Duff."

Mr. Duff felt of his injured eye and contented himself with rolling the other one about him in an amazed manner.

"This is not John Cutter," said the Liar; "it's"—

"Is 'e tall, or ain't 'e?" demanded Mr. Pitcher, indignantly.

"Yes," said the Liar; "but"—

"Now look a-'ere," grumbled Mr. Duff, finding his tongue. "Is 'e smooth shaved? Now I say, is 'e smooth shaved, or ain't 'e?"

"Perhaps 'e ain't got light hair," said Mr. Pitchers with biting sarcasm.

"Silence!" screamed the Liar. "As I'm a dead man, this is not my assassin. It is Lord Dangerford."

"Duff," said Mr. Pitchers, fixing an accusing eye on his partner, "Duff, you're a bloomink hass!"

"Pitchers," said Mr. Duff in injured tones, "if I'm a bloomink hass, you're another."

I saw the Comédienne and Little Bobby sneaking away together, and a great light broke in upon me.

"Stop!" I commanded. "Girls, you wrote that letter. Don't attempt to deny it."

"Oh, did you? Did you? Bless you!" said the delighted ex-victim of John Cutter's bloody intentions, including both Little Bobby and the Comédienne in a single embrace." Bless you! Then I'm not a dead man. Messrs. Pitchers and Duff, it's all a mistake. I'm not a dead man. Send in your bill."

"If you can find the key to those things," said Lord Dangerford, "I'll unlock you and you can go back to Scotland Yard.

After Mr. Pitchers and Mr. Duff had addressed to each other various uncomplimentary epithets with the apparent desire of conciliating His Lordship, the key of the handcuffs was finally found and the detectives were once more in full possession of their lawful rights and privileges.

"Sir!" said Daffy, as the Liar cast a reassuring smile upon her, "your presence is distasteful to me."

"Excuse me for being alive," retorted the Liar, sullenly.

"Whether you are alive or dead is not of the slightest consequence to me."

"You act as though you owned the whole show."

"No I don't," said Daffy, getting in her triumphant last word, "or you wouldn't be in it!"

Then I knew that all was well with us again.

CHAPTER X

"It is most extraordinary; I don't understand it at all."

"London is full of extraordinary things," said the American Friend. "To which particular extraordinary thing do you refer?"

He had called at the close of a matinee performance to take me to one of the "Historical Dinners," as he called them, which he had planned for my enlightenment on Saturday evenings between the two performances of that most trying day of the week.

"Their shocking ignorance, or their criminal indifference,—one is as bad as the other,—regarding some of their most famous men," I said.

"Don't be unjust, my dear. You forget about our visit to the site of the old Globe Theatre, and the haunts of Shakespeare and Ben Jonson; and how everybody we met"—

"Oh, I except Ben Jonson," I replied,

125

"though I don't understand why he should be remembered to the exclusion of his betters. As for Shakespeare, he is one of those exceptions which prove all rules."

"It was only a week ago that we dined at the Cheshire Cheese," objected the American Friend; "and you must have observed how general is the desire to do honor to the memory of Dr. Johnson."

"It is all on account of that truckling, garrulous old villain Boswell," I retorted, indignantly. "Boswell reminds me of the moon during an eclipse of the sun. I tell you, Boswell is the chief literary crime of the Nineteenth Century—or of the Eighteenth, whichever it was."

"If you mean Thackeray"—

"Oh, Thackeray, by all means," I retorted in my most sarcastic manner. "If Thackeray had lived to picture the generation of snobs his Book of Snobs created, his fame would endure throughout the ages. Why the very cabman who drove me to the theatre this afternoon pointed out the house where General Newcombe lived, and declared that he knew Pendennis 'by 'eart, mum.'"

We were standing outside the stage door

waiting for the cab which the American Friend
had signaled. My patient guide to the literary
haunts of London smiled down upon me in-
dulgently.

"Come," said he, "let us look the situation
squarely in the face; who is this Sun of yours
which poor Boswell eclipses when he holds up
before it the mellow disc of Dr. Johnson?"

"How can you, an American, ask?" I demanded, almost with indignation. "Of whom
are the very sign boards eloquent? Why does
the sight of St. Paul's Churchyard make one
feel like shedding tears? Who made the Temple, its Inns and the Law Courts realities even
to the farmer boys of Minnesota? Why did I
nearly fall off the top of a 'bus yesterday in my
anxiety to catch a glimpse of Lincoln's Inn
Fields? What makes the very name of Fleet
Street eloquent? How is it that the large sign
at the entrance to the grounds of St. Maryle-
bones' Hospital should possess a fascination
which not even the remnant of Whitehall ex-
erts, though it seems to bring us face to face
with famous court beauties and the most heartless fop that ever sat on the throne of England?
Whose magic pen was it that made these loca-
tions familiar in the remotest American village

—almost on every American farm? Was it Thackeray's?"

Again the American Friend smiled upon me. I detected secret approval in it. As we entered the cab he nodded to the driver and said: "Jimpson's."

"Come," he said, "we will go and have a chat with the only man in London who remembers Dickens."

Every Londoner—every visitor to London whose stomach asserts its supremacy over its neighboring vital organs—knows Jimpson's. At Jimpson's you don't have to throw yourself on the merciful generosity of an autocrat inhabiting some distant part of the establishment who does the carving. This functionary, wearing a bland smile of welcome, and armed with a large, keen knife, pushes up to your elbow on a wheeled table the whole huge steaming joint from which you have elected to take the major portion of your repast. Having served you with a juicy slice large enough to fill two stomachs of the capacity of your own, he retires, but does not make his exit. No; from a discreet distance he takes observations of the progress you are making, ready on the first indication that your capacity is rising to the opportunity to bear down upon you again with the bland smile, the large keen knife and the wheeled table groaning under the steaming joint. If ever a diner out was seen to "swell wisibly before one's werry eyes" that spectacle undoubtedly had Jimpson's for its scene of action.

Accordingly, one may not expect to be accommodated with an exclusive table at Jimpson's. In fact, a disposition so foreign to the Jimpson spirit persisted in at more than two successive visits would, without doubt, result in the offender being denied further enjoyment of Jimpson privileges. Nor would this summary act of justice proceed necessarily from the bland autocrat of the wheeled table and the knife. The offender would read his doom in the outraged glances of the owners of all the capacious stomachs then doing their duty by Jimpson. Entering in the proper Jimpson spirit you seem to see all these noble stomachs extending toward you, figuratively speaking, the hand of good fellowship, as though they would say: "Ah, another one of us. Enter, good Sir Stomach. Your brother stomachs welcome you with joy. Wherever you find a space sufficient to contain you, making due allowance for proper and worthy distention as the meal progresses, there, good Sir Stomach, place yourself, and, notifying your servant, Brain, that your Gastric Juices are ready for action, defy the world ! ''

Such, indeed, seemed to be what the fair, round stomach adjoining the only two vacant places at Jimpson's was endeavoring to express as we entered. We lost no time in accepting the invitation. I noticed immediately that this friendly stomach was surmounted by a large, shaggy head upon the front of which nature had painted a countenance at once intelligent, amiable and exceedingly shrewd. Though it was evident that they were entire strangers the American Friend and this gentleman exchanged cordial greetings as he made room for us. I set this down to the Jimpson atmosphere. The autocrat of the carving knife lost no time in exercising his function on our behalf; nor did we in rising to the opportunity. This latter fact seemed to be noted with special gratification by the white-haired attendant who had welcomed us at the door. Presently he came to our table and busied himself with some unimportant details of the service.

"Good-evening, Charles," said the American Friend; "how are you feeling this evening?"

"Pretty well, sir, for an old man. Goin' on eighty, sir."

"You don't think of retiring, Charles, I hope. Jimpson's wouldn't be Jimpson's without you."

"Thankee, sir. Have a pinch out of the old box, sir?"

The old fellow had taken from his pocket an ancient silver snuff box, which he stroked fondly with his wrinkled hand and then offered it to the American Friend. I noticed an amused glance pass between the latter and the shrewd-faced gentleman, whereupon the American Friend said:

"What have we here, Charles? A souvenir? A token of faithful services rendered some great patron of the past? Haven't I seen this box before, Charles?"

"Oh, yes, indeed, sir; the last time you were 'ere, sir."

"Ah, now I remember. This is the box presented to you by Leigh Hunt—or was it Thackeray?"

"Oh, no, sir; not at all sir. Mr. Hunt was too 'ard up mostly, sir, to give away silver snuff boxes. Mr. Thackeray 'e gave me a pipe, sir—

genooine French briar, sir. Perhaps you'll kindly look at the inscription on the bottom of the box, sir?"

The American Friend took the box and examined it with extreme care, the result of the examination being awaited by its owner with a smile of confident and pleasant anticipation.

"Why, what is this, Charles? Not Dickens! You don't mean that the author of David Copperfield gave you this snuff box?"

"Oh, yes, sir; indeed, sir. His Lordship will tell you that there's no doubt about it. Charles Dickens gave me the box with his own hand, sir, saying as I took it: ''Oping, Charles, that you'll live to sneeze into it till you're a hundred.' Those were 'is hidentical words, sir."

"Quite so," said the shrewd-faced gentleman addressed as "His Lordship." "Charles tells the exact truth." And he returned to his third slice of Southdown saddle of mutton.

My mutton had suddenly lost its charm. I turned eagerly to the owner of the snuff box:

"Did you see Dickens often? Did he make a habit of dining here?"

"Oh, yes, mum. 'E was very fond of coming 'ere for his bit o' mutton and lettuce salad. I always waited on him. Mr. Dickens, Mr. Thack-

eray, Mr. Hunt, sometimes Mr. DeQuincey—
though Mr. DeQuincey's stomach was 'ardly up
to our 'earty serving, mum—Mr. Forster and
Mr. Leach, always 'ad to 'ave ' Charles ' wait on
'em. Oh, yes, indeed, mum."

"But Dickens. What was he like? What
did he say? Didn't all the others seem to hang
on his words as though afraid to miss a precious
syllable ? "

" 'E was not very tall, mum—about medium
—with a full beard, and very active on 'is feet.
'E warn't very solid in 'is conversation, mum.
Mr. Thackeray, now"—

"Never mind about Thackeray," I said, somewhat rudely, I fear; "I am an American,
Charles. In America there are a hundred who
know and love Dickens to one who has even
heard of Thackeray."

"So the Hamericans all tell me," said the old
waiter, shaking his grey head dubiously. "You
see, mum, you don't 'ave any haristocracy in
America."

"Charles, Charles," said I, "how can you
prate about the aristocracy, you who had the
great honor of knowing the creator of Little
Nell, poor Paul Dombey, Smike, Dick Swivel-

ler, Newman Noggs, Peggoty, the Cheeryble Brothers, and all their dear companions?"

Charles looked at the American Friend, as though at a loss what answer to make.

"Characters in Dickens' novels, Charles— The Old Curiosity Shop, Dombey and Son, Nicholas Nickleby, and so on."

"Certainly, mum," said the owner of the souvenir snuff box, brightening up; "'e always gave me one of his books as soon as they was out. They're all, every one, on my shelves at 'ome. Some day I shall read 'em; certainly, mum, most certainly. 'Ave a bit of snuff out of the old box, sir, I must be goin' to look after the other guests, sir."

Solemnly and with becoming reverence the American Friend and the shrewd-faced gentleman took small pinches of the contents of the souvenir snuff box, sneezed respectfully, and dropped each a silver half crown into the expectant palm of the man who knew Dickens, who had all of the great author's novels "on his shelves," and had never seen the inside of one of them! I felt that my face was red with indignation.

"Well," said the American Friend, "you've met the man who knew Dickens."

"And what is more," I retorted sharply, "I am now convinced that he represents the average literary intelligence of his countrymen. The other night when our flag and the Union Jack floated side by side at the theatre, and we poor painted creatures of the stage were cheered by the audience because we belonged to the nation that had given Dewey, the greatest of naval heroes, to the world, I thought how natural and proper it would be for these great sister nations—the one that produced Nelson and the one that produced Dewey—to stand shoulder to shoulder henceforth, for civilization and humanity. But now "—I paused, confused by the quizzical, yet approving glance the shrewd-faced gentleman was bending upon me.

"But now?" he repeated, encouragingly.

"But now I am in grave doubt," I resumed, half defiantly. "How could we have entire confidence in a nation that only half knows, and does not understand nor appreciate at all, its own Dickens?"

"My dear young lady," said the shrewd-faced gentleman, rising from the table, "you will think better of us. I hope to live to see the day when America and England do stand shoulder to shoulder, for civilization and humanity, as you well express it, against the rest of the world." He smiled as he was departing, and added: "It is a pity that you, who have such clear perceptions of what is natural, and what is calculated most to benefit humanity, should not bend your talent toward their realization—instead of allowing yourself to become incensed over small differences of temperament."

"Ah, I always felt it in my bones," said the American Friend, gazing upon me admiringly.

"What have you always felt in your bones?" I asked.

"That you were born to shine in diplomatic circles, my dear. The expression you wrung from the gentleman who has just now left us would create the biggest kind of a sensation in Washington. If you are a patriot—if you truly love your country—all the ships in our navy could not accomplish more than you would in having that expression made publicly."

"I'll do it," I said excitedly, feeling a sudden presentiment of the influence I was so shortly to wield in high places. "Who was the gentleman that just left us?"

"The Marquis of Silsbury," said the American Friend.

CHAPTER XI

In view of my great patriotic ambition inspired by the Marquis of Silsbury's eloquent words, I felt justified in breaking my promise to Prue. Upon her representation that our small savings were not only exhausted but that I was in debt to the management to the amount of nearly a hundred pounds, I had agreed to deny myself the Ascot Cup extravagance. Now I felt that it would be criminal in me to miss such an opportunity of becoming further acquainted with the flower of the British aristocracy. Certainly, without such an acquaintance all my efforts in the diplomatic line would be in vain. Besides, what other chance, half so encouraging, was I likely to have to meet the Marquis himself and lay the foundations of a friendship that would be useful—yes, useful to my country !

"Prue," I said in my firmest tones, as I finished my coffee, " Prue, I am very sorry, but I have a duty to perform which requires my presence at the races to-day."

" You have also a duty which you owe to the

137

green grocer, and another to the butcher," said Prue, with equal firmness.

"The green grocer and the butcher will have to wait, Prue. It is their habit to wait. It is their duty to wait, since they charge us for waiting whether we make them wait or not. But our war with Spain is something that cannot be made to wait."

"What has our war with Spain to do with the matter?" I saw with secret satisfaction that Prue's astonishment had disarmed her. So I replied, composedly:

"A word from the Marquis of Silsbury will convince the world that Her Majesty's ships and sailors are ours for the asking; the Marquis of Silsbury will be at the races to-day; I shall induce him to say that word."

Prue opened her mouth once or twice, finally closing it with a snap. It remained closed until, dressed and ready to enter the waiting hansom, I said:

"How much ready money have we, Prue?"

"One five-pound note, a shilling and nine pence ha'penny."

"You may keep the shilling and nine pence ha'penny," said I. "Give me the five-pound note. I'll make the Artiste pay the cabman."

I did not tell Prue that as we would be in the generous hands of the American Friend and Teddy—the latter being somewhat celebrated as "the deputy American Friend"—my five-pound note would remain intact for investment on the winner. I felt that Fortune could not be blind to such patriotism as mine, and I pictured to myself Prue's surprise when, on my return, I replenished our lean exchequer from the golden shower of my winnings.

I picked up the Artiste at her house. The American Friend and Teddy, his deputy, were waiting for us at the station. A little more than an hour later we were seated comfortably on a drag stationed within easy view of the Royal Box.

We were not early. The Enclosure was crowded and brilliant with the exquisite gowns of aristocratic ladies, among which stalked solemnly the black frock coats and high hats of their husbands and lovers. There was no difficulty in distinguishing the husbands from the lovers. The high hats told the story. On the heads of the husbands they were dignifiedly upright, as became hats accustomed to rule British domestic hearths; on the heads of the lovers they leaned tenderly over the gayest of the Ascot gowns.   Oh, indiscreet top hats !

Presently I caught sight of a top hat that was not so easily classified.   It was in close proximity to one of the gayest gowns in the Enclosure, but it neither tilted tenderly above it nor yet stood proudly upright.   Soon the mystery was cleared away ; the gown covered disdainful shoulders of the Countess Pipedreme, and the hat the indifferent head of Lord Dangerford.   One sees some things most clearly at a distance.   I became suddenly aware that the indifference expressed in the attitude of His Lordship's hat related to Countess Pipedreme ; I already knew that the Countess' shoulders were never so disdainful as when in my presence.   It was plain that His Lordship had noticed our arrival and that the Countess was not anxious to share his attentions with one in my humble sphere.

Meanwhile the Artiste was chattering away conveying volumes of information regarding the titled personages present.   The Artiste was no stranger to London.   This was her third visit; but from her familiarity with the outward aspect of nobility one would have imagined her a native.

"Over there by the Royal Box," she was saying; "the lady in pale grey covered with embroidery, in the dark blue bonnet,—that is the Duchess of Devonshire. Doesn't the Duchess of Westminster look sweet? That is she in the dark velvet with jeweled embroideries. The handsome lady in black with white showing through the lace insertion is the Duchess of Manchester. Oh, and there is the Duchess of Portland—the one in black lace over white. You may recognize her by the bunch of pink malmaisons she carries. She always carries them. I wonder why. I shall find out sometime."

"Who is the lady in dark blue with the purple boa?" I asked. "I'm sure I've met her somewhere."

"You haven't met her, my dear," replied the Artiste. "You've simply seen her pictures in the newspapers at home so often that you imagine you've met her. That is the American wife of Lord Randolph Churchill. Oh, here comes Lord Dangerford. My dear, do you know that he is heir to the title and estates of the old Marquis of Tidewater?"

No; I now heard for the first time of His Lordship's exalted prospects. Now I understood. Countess Pipedreme was ambitious to become a Marchioness. How the example of Lord Randolph Churchill must worry her!

"And Countess Pipedreme is tacked onto him as usual," said Teddy, with a grin in my direction.

"Who is Countess Pipedreme?" I asked. "Nobody seems to know where she comes from."

"That's because she comes from nowhere," said Teddy.

"I wonder where she got her title," I said; "I never heard of a Count Pipedreme."

"She dreamed it," said Teddy. "Of all the numerous ways of obtaining titles that is the easiest."

At this instant there was a sudden movement toward the Royal Box.

"The Prince!" exclaimed the Artiste.

The Royal procession was smaller and duller than I had been led to anticipate. The only bright thing about it was the scarlet-coated escort of Horse Guards. But I thought the Princess of Wales beautiful. As she smiled and bowed to the Duchesses of Portland and Manchester it did not seem to me that she could be a day over thirty; and how sweet was her expression! She wore black embroidered in white, with a mauve boa, and a mauve bonnet with a red rose tucked in at the back. Beside her was Princess Christian in a covert coat with a dark skirt. The Duke of Connaught was with the Prince. As the procession approached the Royal Box I heard the Artiste saying:

"The Prince looks handsome and amiable, doesn't he. But what is the reason, I wonder, for that odd movement of the muscles of his face and of his right eye—almost as though he was winking good-naturedly at some one?"

"That's not difficult to explain," said the ever-ready Teddy. "For more than forty years the Prince has spent so much of his time lifting his hat and bowing and smiling from his carriage that the motions have become mechanical."

The Prince of Wales and the Duke of Connaught were soon seen moving about the Enclosure talking to their friends. I saw the Prince smilingly return Lord Dangerford's diffident salutation. Then His Lordship, with Countess Pipedreme still as his elbow, came up to our drag and shook hands cordially. The Countess merely nodded coolly, saying an indistinct word or two, then, half turning toward the Royal Box, appeared oblivious to the conversation that followed.

"This is an unexpected pleasure," said Lord Dangerford. "I imagined you too serious-minded to think of wasting a day amid such frivolities as these."

"My conscience is easy," said I. "Am I not justified in my frivolity by the examples of the Prince of Wales, the Marquis of Silsbury, Lord Dangerford"—

"But the Marquis of Silsbury is not here," interrupted His Lordship, smiling. "Report says His Lordship is detained by pressing affairs of state."

"Oh, I'm so sorry. I would not have come if I had known this."

His Lordship looked chagrined, and I noticed by the curve of the Countess' cheek that she was smiling.

"You must know, Lord Dangerford," I hastened to add, "that I am here for precisely the same reason that the Marquis of Silsbury remains away."

"Affairs of state? Really, Miss Casino, I am not surprised. A little unofficial diplomacy on your part might do your country a deal of good just now."

"Are you in earnest?" I asked, eagerly.

"Perfectly."

I thought I noticed the Countess prick up her ears at this.

"And I am right in seeking an opportunity to gain the friendship of the Marquis of Silsbury?"

"You could not do better. You know that it is not necessary for any official action to be taken. An unofficial word spoken in public by the right person—a word showing that the sympathies of Her Majesty's subjects are with their kinsmen, the Americans,—would have an effect on the Powers almost as great as the signing of a treaty of alliance."

I gave His Lordship a look of gratitude. "Oh, dear Lord Dangerford, how glad I am that you think so. And do you really think that a poor girl, with nothing to recommend her except a patriotism as strong as that of any of her sisters or brothers, could exert an influence that would help"—

"Yes. Her wit might discover the place and the opportunity; and her influence would prevent the opportunity from being missed through indolence or forgetfulness."

"Lord Dangerford," I said, "may I have the great advantage of your introduction to the Marquis of Silsbury?"

Countess Pipedreme turned sharply about and fixed her round eyes on His Lordship's troubled countenance.   He replied hesitatingly:

"Believe me, Miss Casino, there are reasons —just at present—reasons which you could hardly appreciate, why I cannot "—

"My dear," broke in the Countess, almost cordially, "don't let that trouble you.   There are plenty of others who will be glad to do you this service—as I dare say you will discover before the day is over.   Lord Dangerford, shall we rejoin the Duchess?"

His Lordship bowed to me with, I thought, a flash of appeal in his eyes, and, giving his arm to the Countess, they made their way toward the Royal Box.   The Countess stopped on the way to say a confidential word to the Earl of Drippingeaves.   During the next ten minutes I saw her bright-colored bonnet bobbing about here and there.   She seemed to be in high favor with most of the young noblemen in the Enclosure.

"How do you do, Miss Casino?   Delighted, I'm sure."

The Earl of Drippingeaves was standing beside our drag reaching up to me a set of slender, jeweled fingers.   We shook hands.

"Awfully glad to meet you," said the Earl. "Been trying to see you for a week. Want you to come to our reception at the Club. Exclusive. Best people only. The Duchess of Edgecombe, Lord Dangerford, the Honorable Mrs. Pebblestone, the Marquis of Silsbury. Perhaps you'll sing something—Lady Dunstable and Countess Pipedreme contribute to the programme, you know."

"On what evening?" I asked. "Perhaps I can come after the theatre."

"Say the word, Miss Casino, and I'll call for you. Delighted."

"If you will present me to the Marquis of Silsbury," said I, "I'll sing as much as you like. But I wouldn't think of troubling Your Lordship to call for me."

"No trouble, really."

I shook my head. I had heard a great deal about the Earl's habit of personally conducting ladies of the stage.

"Cruelty, thy name is woman!" said the Earl with a languishing glance.

But I sent him about his business. And soon I was heartily glad of it, for, during the next half hour, four of the most dissipated young noblemen in London, who still, somehow, hung onto the skirts of respectability, called on me, one at a time, with pressing invitations to suppers of dubious propriety, to excursions to places I had never heard of, and even to midnight revels in some gentleman's chambers. And when the last of this delectable procession had thrown out the bait of an introduction to the Marquis of Silsbury, the scales suddenly fell from my eyes.

The Countess Pipedreme was striking at my reputation with the weapon I had thoughtlessly placed in her hand. Very well, I now knew how to parry the stroke. I would be taken suddenly ill on the night of the Earl's "reception," which I now divined was the polite name he had given to an orgy planned to meet the occasion. Of course the Marquis of Silsbury would not be there. I could picture to myself the hypocritical sorrow with which the Earl of Drippingeaves would announce the Marquis' regrets.

Having nipped this little conspiracy in the bud, my spirits rose several degrees. Bookmakers were moving about naming the odds they offered on the horses now about to start in the great race of the day. I opened my purse and beckoned to one of them.

Teddy seized me by the arm. "Don't do that," he said.

"Why not?"

"These fellows are welchers."

"What is a welcher?"

"A dishonest 'bookie.' He'll take your money, and when you've lost he'll come back politely and tell you so."

"But if I win?"

"You can't win."

"But if my horse comes in first?"

"That doesn't matter."

"If my horse comes in first I win."

"I say you can't win," repeated Teddy, earnestly.

"Why not?"

"Because the welcher can't lose. He can't afford to. If your horse comes in first your 'bookie' 'welches'—that is to say, he forgets all about you. You never see him again."

"Do you mean to say that the law"—

"First catch your welcher."

"I shouldn't think his life would be safe in such a crowd."

"It isn't," said Teddy, with a grin; "but he takes his chances."

"But I want to bet," said I.

"All right, I'll place your money for you."

"Thank you so much."

I gave him my five-pound note. "Masque II. to win; Bay Ronald for place; half on each."

Teddy whistled. "Did you dream it?"

"I like their looks," said I. "And look at the odds."

"If they· get in at all it will be sometime to-morrow," said Teddy.

"Nevertheless it goes," said I.

Teddy whistled again. He leaned over and spoke to one or two sporty persons standing near our drag, but didn't leave his seat.

"Well, you've a fighting chance," he said, finally. "It will be a good haul. I wish I had your nerve."

"But why don't you place my money?" I said. "The horses are at the post."

"Your money's placed," said Teddy.

I wasn't quite sure, but I thought he winked at the American Friend.

At that instant they were off. It didn't seem to me that I breathed until it was over. What would I say to Prue?

"Just as I said," remarked Teddy, with a compassionate glance; "your horses will be in sometime to-morrow."

"It is some satisfaction to know," said I,
"that my five-pound note will not help to en-
rich a welcher."

"Yes," assented Teddy. "You could look a
long time before you would find a more honest
man than the one that's pocketed your five
pounds."

The American Friend laughed.

"I'm glad of it," said I; "I'd like to meet
him."

"You have," said Teddy. And he took from
his vest pocket my bank note and offered it to
me with his best bow.

"But if I had won?"

"Teddy would have paid up like a man,"
said the American Friend.

"I knew you couldn't win," said Teddy,
modestly, trying to force the money on me.

Of course I couldn't accept it. But neither
could I prevent Teddy from taking us all to the
Tower of Babel to dinner on our return from
the races; so that, financially speaking, I had
the better of him, after all.

This merry ending of a day, which at one
time threatened me with serious loss of reputation through the machinations of Countess
Pipedreme, convinced me that after all old

friends, however humble, should be clung to and cherished to the sacrifice, if necessary, of apparently the most brilliant prospects.

But I hadn't the slightest intention of abandoning my designs upon the Marquis of Silsbury for all that.

CHAPTER XII

MY Ascot Cup experience had an amusing
sequel, which, for the space of twenty-four
hours, rendered me oblivious to my diplomatic
responsibilities. Sometimes when I think of
the frequency with which my naturally serious
mind is diverted from its most worthy pursuits
by the odd and humorous aspects of humanity
that come under my observation I almost fear
that these memoirs, instead of challenging the
respect of the thoughtful, will have general acceptance only in the Pickwickian sense. However, I shall be consoled by the reflection that
I have at all times held the mirror up to nature, and that truth is mighty and will prevail.

On the Saturday night following Cup Day I
was standing back of the scenes dressed and
ready for the curtain to rise on the last act.

" My dear," said the Comédienne, approaching from the direction of the stage door, " did
you lose your purse at the races ? "

" Yes," I replied ; " Mr. Squibs made a note
of it in the *Gazette* this morning."

"Well, there's a very agitated person at the door who insists on seeing you about it."

"Perhaps the honest man found my purse," said I. "There wasn't sixpence in it, but he deserves a reward just the same."

The Comédienne and I went to the door and had the man admitted to the stage. He was a lank, long-faced person of the shabby genteel class. There were lines in his face which I readily interpreted as meaning that he was the father of six, and the husband of one who stood on the letter of her marital rights. But there was the ghost of a twinkle in his eye and an upward turn to the corners of his mouth that bore pathetic evidence of his determination not to succumb wholly to the weight of his domestic burden. Just now, however, it was quite plain that the burden was at its heaviest.

"I am Miss Casino," I said, gently, giving him my hand with a feeling of sincere sympathy.

"At larst!" exclaimed the poor creature, with a look of ecstasy, as he took my hand in both his own and let fall a tear upon it. "At larst Hi'm 'olding 'er little 'and in me werry own!"

The Comédienne laughed in the poor fellow's face, as I drew my hand hastily away.

"If you have come to return my purse, my good man, I will reward you," said I.

" Halas! no, Miss. Would to 'eavings I 'ad." And the look of ecstasy with which he had taken my hand gave place to one of misery. " Would to 'eavings I 'ad, Miss."

" Please state your business, then," said I; " the curtain will go up in a minute."

" Halas! she knows me not," said the strange creature, regarding me with mournful eyes. " Notwithstanding the 'avoc she 'ave created in this 'eart of 'earts, 'er blessed heyes knows me not!"

"I never saw you before in all my life," I said in amazement.

" True," said the man, shaking his head sadly, " she speaks but the truth. Hi did not send the picture. Hi thought of the little 'one in Clapham and Hi only sent the letters. Halas! the letters! Woe, woe, the letters!"

" Do you mean that you wrote to me, sir? "

He looked at me as though doubting the evidence of his ears.

"She arsks if Hi wrote to 'er. Oh, 'eavings!"

"Oh," I exclaimed, a sudden light breaking in upon me, "are you the one who signed himself, 'The Galleryite'?"

"Being poor in this world's goods," said the man with dignity, "Hi sat in the gallery. Being honest as well as poor, Hi signed myself 'The Galleryite.' Ha man may be poor and honest and still 'ave a 'eart, Miss. 'E may 'ave a little 'ome in Clapham, and a missus with a temper which ain't wot it once was, halas! and 'alf a dozen holive branches, and still 'ave a 'eart, Miss—a 'eart to be stirred by youth and beauty, halas!"

"There's no harm done," I said, cheerfully; "you can have the letters back."

"'Eavings! Hi breathes again! Hall of them, Miss?" The poor man seemed immensely relieved.

"All of them. Give me your address and I will mail them to you."

"And they warn't in the purse she lost at the races?"

"No, not one of them, I assure you," I said, eager to relieve the poor man's mind. But far from exhibiting relief he shook his head sadly, clasped his hands and raised his eyes, saying:

"Halas! hall in vain! Hi 'oped she might

'ave carried one in her buzzum. False 'ope.
Halas, halas ! "

" Sir," I said, with indignation, " I never
carry the letters of strangers in my bosom.
Nor in my purse either. I have said that if
you will give me your address I will return all
of yours without loss of time."

" Halas ! Too late, too late ; oh, the little
'ome in Clapham ! The Missus knows hall—
hall ! "

" Then you were a fool for telling her," I
said, quite out of patience with the man.

" Hi felt that Hi 'ad to, Miss, halas ! "

" If you are such an idiot you ought to know
better than to write letters at all."

" You 'ave no hidea of the Missus. Indeed
no, none whatever. Hi tells the Missus of me
guilt and she remembers it a year; Hi lets 'er
find it out, and she remembers it forever. It's
hall over then, halas ! When Hi read in the
Gazette this morning—Hi always takes it with
me coffee—that you 'ad lost your purse at the
races, Miss, Hi pictured to myself the ruin of
a 'appy 'ome in Clapham when the finder of the
purse would take it to the *Gazette* hoffice, and
the paper would print my letters for hidentifi-
cation. Halas ! Hi never thought of the letters

being hanywhere else, Miss. And so Hi con-
fessed hall to the Missus, halas, halas!"

"And what did the Missus do about it?"
asked the Comédienne.

"Halas! she took me latchkey, and made
me a 'ard bed on the floor of the coal 'ouse."

"Oh, that's too bad," said I. "If you can
think of anything I can do to straighten out
matters I'll be only too glad."

At this my Galleryite brightened percepti-
bly. "Thank you, Miss. The Missus was on
the stage once 'erself. To-morrow is Sunday.
Perhaps now you could find it in your 'eart to
call at our 'umble 'ome in the afternoon. The
Missus would happreciate the hattention, and
hall would be forgiven. To be sure the holive
branches hall 'as 'ooping cough; but 'ooping
cough is catching honly to them as hasen't 'ad it."

"I've had it," said the Comédienne. "Accept this good man's invitation and let me go
with you."

Now that the tragic element had been elimi-
nated from the incident I was no less eager
than the Comèdienne to seize this opportunity
for a further investigation of London social
conditions. So I held out my hand to my
Galleryite again, and said:

" Very well, you can expect us at about four
in the afternoon."
" Oh, thank you, Miss. The Missus will be
proud to hextend the 'ospitalities of our 'umble
'ome. But "— He hesitated plainly embarrassed.
" Well?" said I, encouragingly.
"Hi would take it as a favor, Miss, if you
would destroy the letters. The Missus made
me a promise to 'ave 'em sent to 'er. But if
you 'ad halready destroyed 'em "—
I promised to report to "the Missus" the
total destruction of the compromising documents. Having thanked me again, with tears
in his eyes, and given me his address, the poor
man threw a lingering glance about the stage,
sighed deeply, and departed.
One needs to have had experience of the life
back of the footlights to realize that such characters as the Galleryite actually exist. It is
extraordinary the number of husbands and
fathers in humble circumstances there are who
seek to relieve the sordid monotony of domestic
life by indulging in some little secret romance.
It is fortunate for such men, and for those
dependent upon them, that they so generally
restrict attentions of this kind to ladies of the

stage. Members of my profession become so accustomed to this sort of thing that letters and gifts of flowers and jewels make a very small impression on them; except, of course, when the writer or the sender of gifts establishes his right to be considered in the light of a legitimate suitor. The romance-seeking husband and father may therefore indulge his epistolary fancy to his heart's content. A single glance. from a practiced eye at one of his effusions fixes his status. He would seem to be a masculine paradox if he were not so numerous. He will write anonymous love letters of the most fervid character without dreaming of any act of disloyalty to his home, just as romantic young girls write them without any hope or possibility of reply. I will not speak of the class of men who go through life always fluctuating between duty and some secret attachment. A menace hangs perpetually over those who are entitled to the love and protection of such a man. But in the case of the Galleryite, as you have observed, the first suggestion of menace to his domestic peace sent him scurrying frantically back to the bibs and apron strings.

The one feature of the Galleryite's case that puzzled me was explained when he said that

his wife had been an actress. I then understood how she could perform the apparently
unfeminine act of inviting to her house the re-
cipient of her husband's love letters. Her experiences while on the stage had long ago enabled her to form the same conclusions I have
just expressed. The Comédienne agreed with
me that we might expect to find the " Missus "
of the " Little 'ome in Clapham " an agreeable
hostess, serene in the consciousness of her ability to keep her spouse's feet in the straight and
narrow path.

The day was so pleasant that even Clapham
was attractive. The Galleryite's house was
one of a long row of diminutive dwellings set
primly in the exact centre of a diminutive plot
of ground, each having a diminutive front porch
at the top of a short flight of steps, and the
front windows of each looking out upon precisely identical attempts at landscape garden-
ing on the smallest scale imaginable. It was
impossible to question the sobriety of the neighborhood. No intoxicated householder, returning to his home on a dark night, would have
more than one chance in twenty of escaping
scandalous intrusion upon some other householder's domestic privacy. The Sabbath calm

of the street seemed almost puritanical. The few children to be seen on the diminutive front porches were sedate and clean in their Sunday frocks and trousers. About the Galleryite's house, however, there were no evidences of life.

"It is the whooping cough," said the Comédienne; "the good people are afraid of infecting the neighborhood."

Even as we mounted the steps ominous sounds from within verified the Comédienne's surmise. We waited until six paroxysms of coughing, each followed by that audibly spasmodic effort to recover exhausted breath so terrifying to the uninitiated, had informed us that the "olive branches" had passed safely through another crisis, and then rang the bell. The flushed face and the watery eyes of the little girl who opened the door served to identify her with the concert which had reached our ears on the front porch.

"Step into the parlor, if you please," she said, politely; "mother will be down in a moment."

There was a stair leading to the upper story, and under it another leading to the basement dining-room. The latter was guarded by a balustrade which fronted the open parlor door, and which we were soon to see put to a most novel and ingenius use. Seated in a row in the

parlor were the five other olive branches,
three boys and two more little girls, all clean
and neat in their Sunday clothes, ranging in
ages apparently from ten to five. As we entered they all rose, bowed and said politely in
a chorus:

"How — do — you — do? Won't — you —
pleased—be—seated? Mother—will—be—here
—in—a—moment." Whereupon they all resumed their seats.

"I can sympathize with you, my dears," began the Comédienne, affably; "when I was ten
years old I had a terrible attack of the whooping cough. But "—

But the Comédienne had neglected to remember the intimate relationship between the name
and the deed which distinguishes this malady.
The unfortunate suggestion was instantly acted
upon. The eldest little girl began the fugue
form of whooping chorus (*presto accelerando*)
in which the others took up their parts at regular intervals until all were presently whooping
at once in a grand finale. But before the hyp-
notic infection had reached the youngest little
boy a shrill command, proceeding apparently
from the adjoining room, added a new and astonishing feature to the programme.

"Emmy, Charles, Susannah, the banister! Run to the banister, all of you!" commanded the voice.

Instantly the six children, purple in the face, doubled up with their paroxysm of coughing, scurried into the hall and hung themselves in a row over the basement stair rail, like so many bags of meal.

"My goodness gracious!" ejaculated the Comédienne. "Why do they do that? The little dears will fall downstairs."

But the conundrum was already furnishing its own answer. The support which the stair rail gave to the heaving little chests and stomachs rendered the paroxysms less severe. The chorus of whoops was approaching a leisurely and comfortable conclusion.

"A splendid idea," said the Comédienne; "I'll make a note of it for future reference."

While the children were still doubled over the rail, the door of the adjoining room opened and a stately figure clad in black silk trimmed with jet beads entered and held out a cordial hand to each of us.

"Thank you so much for coming," said the wife of my Galleryite. "The sight of you recalls the dear old days at Drury Lane."

"You of course understand about the letters," I began, anxious to have the embarrassing part of the interview over. "You have been an actress, and doubtless, yourself, have received"—

"Bushels of them," laughed Mrs. Robinson. "Bless you, I know all about it. While I was playing Oberon in 'A Midsummer Night's Dream'—you wouldn't believe it to look at me now, would you?—Mr. Robinson wrote me at least a hundred before I paid any attention to him at all, though at that time he had excellent prospects." The mother of the olive branches sighed gently and gave the six small figures still doubled over the stair rail a loving glance.

"Those your husband addressed to me were anonymous I assure you," I hastened to say. "I couldn't have discovered the indentity of the writer if I had wished to—which of course I didn't. It was only the accident of the lost purse, and your husband's anxiety that"—

"Bless your heart, don't you worry. I know John Robinson. He will keep up his habit of writing letters to actresses; but, bless you, he never forgets his family for a minute. Did he say in his letters to you that your eyes were like stars?"

"Yes," I answered, wonderingly.

"Did he say that your feet were like rose petals whose weight scarcely disturbed the tender blades of grass upon which they fell?"

"His exact words."

"Of course," laughed Mrs. Robinson. "Did he say that your hair was like the mist that veils the sun when it rises from its bed in the sea?"

"He did, and I thought it a very pretty sentiment."

"So did I when he wrote it to me. And I suppose he wrote that your glorious face had the dazzling beauty of the sun when the mists had cleared away?"

I nodded assent, and then Mrs. Robinson, the Comédienne and I burst into a hearty laugh at the expense of all sentimental married men who write letters to footlight favorites.

"Still," said I, beginning to feel myself on terms of intimacy with the Robinson family, "you took away his latchkey."

"Yes; it won't do to pretend you don't care, you know."

"And made him sleep on a hard bed in the coal house?"

"No," laughed Mrs. Robinson, "I only

threatened him with the coal house. One must preserve some sort of discipline in managing a husband."

The six small Robinsons now returned to the parlor, the chorus of whoops having sent back its last faint echo from the basement.

"Dearies," said their mother, smiling fondly upon them, "go into the sitting-room and play. Mother's engaged with company."

The children obeyed. Then Mrs. Robinson rose and said, with a laugh in her eyes:

"My husband wishes to make you a little present—for a souvenir of this occasion."

She opened the same door by which she had entered the parlor and said:

"John, dear?"

There was a shuffling sound from the next room, and then my Galleryite entered with a book in his hand, looking sheepish enough, though infinitely less worried than when he called at the theatre. For at least once in her life the Comédienne was at a loss what to say or do. As for me the novelty of the situation found me powerless to do more than await developments in silence. Mrs. Robinson took the book from her husband and placed it in my hands.

"With the compliments of John Robinson," she said, smiling mischievously, while putting her arm lovingly through her husband's.

"I—I don't understand," I stammered, looking from one to the other in bewilderment.

"Read the title page," said Mrs. Robinson. Mr. Robinson groaned.

"Radley's Ready Letter Writer," I quoted from the title page of the book, still unenlightened.

"Now kindly turn to page one hundred and nine," said Mrs. Robinson, while Mr. Robinson groaned again.

I did so and quoted the chapter heading:

"Letters from a gentleman to a lady with whom he is in love."

"Refer to the tenth line of the first letter," said Mrs. Robinson.

"Oh, 'eavings! spare me!" groaned Mr. Robinson.

I read: "'Your feet are like rose petals whose weight,'" etc.

"Now the thirteenth line of the third letter," commanded Mrs. Robinson, disregarding the expostulations of her spouse.

"'Your hair is like the mist that veils the sun when'—I understand," I said, closing the book. "Thank you, Mr. Robinson. Your handwriting is fairly good, but large print is easier on the eyes. Thank you very much; I'll accept the book with pleasure."

The Comédienne was convulsed. Mrs. Robinson patted her husband's cheek and even he was presently able to appreciate the joke at his expense without losing sight of its import from the sterner standpoint of discipline.

Our cordial farewells were hastened by another sudden outburst of the whooping chorus, and a second infantile stampede for the friendly balustrade. I gave each little pair of heaving shoulders a friendly pat as we were going out.

"What luck some husbands have," said the Comédienne.

"What excellent sense some wives have," said I.

CHAPTER XIII

CAPTAIN LIVELY BECOMES TROUBLESOME

SPEAKING of letters, by no means all of those I received at the theatre and at my house in St. John's wood disturbed me as little as did those of the Galleryite. As all London and New York know, the character I represented was that of a Salvation Lassie. The value of the character, as my author conceived it for stage purposes, is indicated in the first verse of my principal song, the last two lines applying to the character in the play, and to myself both on and off the stage, equally well:

I find it very difficult to make young men religious,
In saving souls from wickedness the labor is prodigious;
 When I ask them to be good,
  As all young men should be,
 They only say they would
  Be very good to me.
I ask them if they'll follow in the path
  That leads to sweet salvation,
But oh! the effect my argument hath
  Fills me with perturbation.
For when those youths profess
  That the light of faith they see,
They never proceed to follow that light,
  But always follow me.

"I represented a Salvation lassie."—Page 170.

Yes, they always followed me! When they did not pursue me personally, they pursued me with letters. The most unique case of the latter description was that of a British original of my stage character—a London Salvation Lassie who lived in barracks over on the Surrey Side and labored nightly in the slums. She wrote me many disturbing letters, of which the following, an exact copy, is a specimen :

"DEAR FRIEND :

" I cannot tell you how grieved I was when I saw your portrait in the illustrated papers as a parody on the Salvation Army. They do not deserve this. The reason for their existence is the misery and wickedness too often commenced in theatres and music halls, and these poor people are saddled with the wreck and ruin caused by theatrical performances.

" It is not our duty alone to go out and rescue those for whom Christ died. It is yours just as much as any one's. For you have talent and ability; and be sure, dear friend, that however you may pass this life —

Amidst the dim unknown
Standeth God among the shadows
Keeping watch above his own

and to him, one day, must you and I give in our account.

"Tell me the answer to this : What does it profit you to gain the whole world and lose (forever) your own soul?

"I write this with sadness at my heart when I think of how your beauty and talent might be given to God to the salvation of mankind.

"It is good to be great, but it is greater to be good.

"May God bless you.

"Zee Zee.

"May 1, 1898."

I wrote "Zee Zee," making as strong a plea for my profession as I was able, showing how it offered a means of livelihood to many who otherwise, doubtless, would come to the slums in which she labored so unselfishly, and asked her to call upon me. After writing me many other letters, and almost convincing me that I ought to quit my mimic slums for the realities of Whitechapel and Salvation Army barracks, she sent a young man in the costume of a petty officer with a request that I send her as many copies as I could spare of the large lithographs representing me in my famous character. She wanted to hang them up in the different army

barracks, where they would be appropriately
decorative.   At my request the manager of the
theatre sent Zee Zee fifty of these pictures,
and later I experienced the unique sensation of
attending prayer-meeting in a Whitechapel Salvation Army hall upon the walls of which, while
these unselfish people prayed and sang, hung no
less than four full length pictures of myself in
stage costume!   But I never met Zee Zee.

But it was to one of Her Majesty's special
pets—a Life Guardsman—that I was indebted
for my chief epistolary annoyance.   He always
signed his full name—Captain Gerald Lively—
and used the crested stationery of Hyde Park
Barracks.   I would have been inclined, perhaps,
to reward his frankness with my acquaintance,
upon his procuring a proper introduction, had
it not been for his horrible familiarity.   Think
of it!   This was his first letter, copied word for
word:

"DEAR MISS CASINO:
    "Do come and have supper on Guard, at
the Horse Guards, Whitehall, to-morrow after
your play is over.
    "I have not the honor of your acquaintance,
but should like to make it awfully.

"If you cannot come to-morrow do come some other time.

"Yours very sincerely,
"(CAPTAIN) GERALD LIVELY."

I of course paid no attention to this letter, except to preserve it as a curiosity. Imagine my surprise, therefore, when, only three days later, came this piece of impudence:

"DEAR MISS CASINO:

"I am awfully sorry for worrying you with my invitation to supper the other night. But how can you blame me?

"Please will you take pity on me, and give me some other evening, dropping me a line to say when? Ever yours,
"(CAPTAIN) GERALD LIVELY."

These were only the beginning. My silence seemed to serve only as a spur to his zeal. This disposition to overcome insurmountable obstacles, though I have no doubt it is extremely useful to Her Majesty—in India and the Soudan—simply strengthened by determination to convince Captain Lively of his lack of any importance whatever where I was concerned.

When, however, he took to haunting the stage
door, I confess that I trembled. Out of pure
mischief Daffy, the Comédienne, Little Bobby
and an English chorus girl whom we nicknamed
"Sloppy Weather," attempted, night after night
to lure the Captain away from the quarry he
had set his heart on. But he would not condescend to notice them.

I could not understand the strange apathy
of Tommy Atkins on this subject, considering
her passion for red coats and pepper box caps
—the passion that had won for her the name
which had caused her legitimate one to become
almost forgotten. But it appeared that Tommy
Atkins had been thinking, and on the evening
when, as my understudy, she was to make her
first appearance in my part—the management
having decided that it would do me good to
skip a performance occasionally—I discovered
to what purpose.

Tommy Atkins bears quite a strong resemblance to me, in form as well as in features.
An understudy is not expected to invest her
performance with any originality. Often she is
a member of the chorus, and this extra duty is
assigned to her on account of the presumption
that she will be able, in case of an emergency,

to give an acceptable imitation of her principal's performance. It was Tommy Atkins' strong personal likeness to me that procured her this post of honor. Naturally I desired that her resemblance to me in the character should be as close as possible in all details. I therefore assisted her to dress in my own room, and superintended her make-up.

"A little more carmine at the centre of the lips," I said, finally. "Remember the prunes and prisms expression—there, that will do nicely."

"Do I look like you?" asked my understudy.

"You are my breathing image," said I.

Just then Prue came in, snorting with indignation.

"What is the trouble, Prue?"

"Captain Lively, in full uniform and partly intoxicated, has got past Jack at the stage door and insists on seeing you before the performance begins."

"The brute!" I exclaimed. "Prue, do you go and say to Captain Lively that unless he leaves instantly I will have him arrested."

"By whom?" inquired Tommy Atkins, calmly.

"By a policeman," said I. "I will have this

Captain of the Horse Guards taught a lesson in manners."

" Not by a policeman," said Tommy, dabbing a powder puff at her round chin.

" And why not by a policeman, pray? Captain Lively's feelings are not of the slightest consequence to me."

" They are to the Queen, though."

" Do you mean to say," I retorted hotly, " that "—

" Her Majesty's officers are not expected to submit to the dictates of policemen," interrupted our authority on British military customers, composedly ; " and—well, the policemen of London are not fools."

" Do you mean," said I, aghast, " that I am at the mercy of this drunken Captain of Horse Guards ? "

" No," said Tommy, drawing herself up to her full height ; " I am here."

Prue and I stared at the girl in amazement.

" Leave Captain Lively to me," Tommy added, confidently ; " I will attend to the case of Captain Lively."

" But—but he won't look at any of the other girls," I said. " I, I alone, am the object of his affections."

"For this evening I am you," replied Tommy Atkins, taking a comprehensive look at herself in the large glass.

"You certainly are," said Prue with emphasis.

"Prue," said Tommy, "do you go and send Captain Lively here. Miss Casino will attend to the proprieties. Oh, pshaw!"—as I made a gesture of dismay—"the manager isn't here."

Prue departed on her mission with evident zest.

"What will you say to Captain Lively, Tommy?" I asked, faintly.

"I shall tell him that if he will promise to be good he may take me to supper after the performance."

"Tommy Atkins!"

"Well, why not?"

"You are a very pretty girl . . . the Captain is intoxicated."

"I am also a thoroughbred American girl—and a total abstainer."

Tommy gave me a queer look. "I haven't denied myself the pleasure of gentlemen's society during my stage career. Tell me, did you ever hear from man or woman a word to my personal discredit?"

"No," said I, "never."

"I was born in Butte, Montana," said Tommy, giving me another of her queer looks. "Until four years ago I had no personal knowledge of any civilization higher than that of mining camps. From my thirteenth to my seventeenth year I sold drinks to miners, cowboys, gamblers and desperadoes, and danced and sung for them. I knew the effect upon those men of every stage of intoxication. Most of them, sober or intoxicated, made love to me. To-day I know that every one of these men now living would defend my character with his life."

Tommy Atkins' eyes sparkled. "Do you know why, dear?"

I shook my head. At that moment the sense of my own weakness and inexperience appalled me.

"Well, this is why." And the girl whipped from some mysterious place of concealment a neat little revolver, which somehow, in her hand, had a terribly business-like appearance.

"Don't, dear," I said, startled. "Is it—is it loaded?"

"It is ALWAYS loaded," said Tommy.

Prue and Captain Lively arriving at this juncture, the revolver disappeared as quickly and mysteriously as it had made its startling entrance upon the scene.

"Aw, Miss Casino, deeply honored, chawmed, chawmed I am suah—haw, haw, haw de do." The Captain was bowing low before Tommy, paying not the slightest attention to me.

"I beg your pardon, Captain Lively," said Tommy, coolly. "I am not Miss Casino. This is Miss Casino"—indicating me.

"Haw, haw, haw," laughed the Captain, hardly so much as glancing at me; "clevah, dooced clevah, 'pon my word."

"Also true," said Tommy. "Ask her."

Captain Lively stuck a bit of glass in his eye and stared at me half drunkenly, half insolently.

"It is true," said I. "I am Miss Casino."

"Haw, haw, haw, dooced clevah, but transparent, you know. Joke might go with lieutenant, haw, haw, but not with captain, by jove, haw, haw, haw." And Captain Lively, turning his back rudely upon me attempted gallantly to raise Tommy's hand to his lips.

My understudy gave him a sharp little slap on the cheek. "No nonsense, now, Captain Lively."

"What, after all these days of constant supplication at—er—at beauty's shrine—that's it, by jove! Beauty's shrine—to be rewarded with blows. Cruel, cruel! Haw, haw, haw. I'll turn the other cheek. I'll turn the other cheek, dooced if I don't, haw, haw, haw."

Captain Lively turned the other cheek. But Tommy stood on her dignity.

"Well, Captain, since you insist that I am Miss Casino, may I ask the object of your call, here at the theatre, thrusting yourself upon the stage against the rules, interrupting the performance of my duty?"

"Oh, come now," said Captain Lively, with an injured air, "what would you have a fellow do, by jove? Half my letters returned unopened, the other half unanswered. Nothing left but storming the citadel, haw, haw, haw. So stormed the citadel, by jove! haw, haw."

"The citadel declines to surrender," said Tommy.

The Captain produced a white handkerchief and held it aloft. "Enemy approaches under flag of truce and asks for conference, haw, haw."

"Request of the enemy is granted," said Tommy, "provided time and place are satisfactory."

"To-night, after the performance ; supper at the barracks, by jove," said the Captain, saluting.

"All on for the first act," yelled the call boy.

"I'll have a hansom at the stage door," said the Captain.

"Agreed," said Tommy.

"No more practical jokes, haw, haw."

"My word is my bond," said Tommy Atkins.

Whereupon the Captain, after another futile attempt to kiss Tommy's hand, departed in high spirits.

My understudy gave a marvelous performance. I witnessed it from the front. I had to pinch myself to make sure whether I was on the stage or in the audience. Captain Lively sat in a stall near the stage, applauding vigorously. He alone was to blame for the deception practiced upon him.

After the performance I went to the door of the waiting hansom with Tommy. The Captain had called for her in person—contrary to the custom common in London of sending an empty cab for the professional guest. He saw us both in our street costumes, but paid no attention to me. So I saw them start with a feeling of genuine relief. After Tommy Atkins' graphic account of her early life in the mining camps I had no doubt that she would prove a match for Captain Lively under any and all circumstances.

CHAPTER XIV

HOW THE WITS UNBEND

" You can't be in earnest," said the American Friend.

" I never was more in earnest in my life," said I. "I am heartily tired of these semi-private exhibitions of the literary and artistic lions of the British metropolis. The Honorable Mrs. Pebblestone's reception given to Mr. Bilkley, the celebrated dramatist, and half a dozen of the other alleged wits of London, was the most dismal affair I ever attended. One would have thought that Mr. Bilkley imagined himself a guest at his own funeral. Neither he nor his famous friends cracked a smile during the entire afternoon. They recited the gloomiest things in melancholy voices, their backbones rigid. It was the same at Lady Dunstable's. When the Duchess of Edgecombe's invitation came, though the guest especially honored was to be Grimshaw, the comedian who convulses his audience nightly at the theatre, I pleaded a previous engagement. I knew how it would be. Grimshaw would arrive punctually, but not until he had laced himself into a straight jacket. No; I care nothing about the wits in their high society aspect. You will kindly present my compliments to the President of the Muses Club and say how much I regret that I am indisposed this evening."

The American Friend listened patiently to my essay on a topic with which he was already, of course, perfectly familiar, and with regard to which he had long before reached a similar conclusion, and then said:

"But the Muses Club is different, my dear. There is where the wits unbend."

"Really?"

"Really. Come, you shall see for yourself."

So we set out for one of the Sunday evening receptions of the Muses Club, a function for which most Londoners have a mighty respect, owing mainly to the fact that one of the founders of the club is no less a personage than His Royal Highness, the Prince of Wales, and partly to the difficulty with which invitations are obtained. It was in the smoking-room of this institution that Sir Henry Irving administered his famous rebuke to a certain sybaritish rival tragedian who spells his particular ART always with capital letters.

Sir Henry one afternoon was smoking a quiet pipe while slowly absorbing a mug of ale. The few members present, respecting the great man's meditations, were silent. Presently entered the Sybarite, his mental infirmity aggravated by a too liberal indulgence in some spiritous compound. Observing his great rival unoccupied, and therefore presumably open to conviction, the Sybarite struck a poetic attitude and said:

"Oh, the degeneracy of these times. Oh, the coarseness of the popular mind—the rudeness of the public conception of ART! Why should one be forced to go on casting his pearls —aye, his PEARLS—before swine? Pearls, I say Pearls." Then fixing an accusing eye on his rival he repeated: "Pearls. Did you hear me say PEARLS, sirrah?"

"Um, uh, eh, ah, pearls, aye, possibly pearls, perhaps pearls, um, ah," grunted Sir Henry reflectively through his nose, while he continued to gaze at vacancy.

"Swine, aye, swine. Did you hear me remark SWINE?"

"Um, ah, swine? Aye, no doubt. Swine, um, uh, ah."

"Oh, for an enlightened public, a public ca-

pable of discriminating between the false and
the true, between the rude and the refined, between—er—between—er—between buncombe
and art. Art, I say ART. Sirrah, did you hear
me say ART?"

"Um, ah, art? Um, ah."

But the subtle satire of the interrogation
point was lost on the Sybarite, who went on:

"Oh, for an opportunity to engrave the principles of true art upon the white page of a
virgin intellect! Oh, for a simple, an unspoiled
public. Aye, a public uncorrupted by the
sophistries of charlatans. Charlatans, I say
CHARLATANS. Sirrah, did you hear me remark,
CHARLATANS?"

"Um, ah, charlatans," assented Sir Henry,
fixing his meditative glance momentarily on the
Sybarite, who was still unconscious of his peril,
though a dozen club members who had gathered
around the rivals were nudging each other in
ecstasy. "Uh, um, aye, charlatans, um, ah, by
all means."

"Oh, for some primitive public, some cluster
of fresh unspoiled minds upon which to graft
the beauteous tree of ART. Oh, for some
island washed by an azure sea where no char-
latan has ever left his insidious footprint. Aye,

an island where the tree of art might thrive un-
trammeled and bear its golden fruit.   Oh, for
an island, I say "—

"Um, ah, an island," said Sir Henry, rising,
and giving the Sybarite a familiar pat on the
shoulder.   "Go to Scilly, my young friend.
Um, ah, go to Scilly.   Go to Scilly and plant
your tree of art among the cabbages."   And
then he stalked from the room.

Some of my American readers will perhaps
appreciate the explanation that the Scilly Is-
lands, which were a part of the mainland in
the time of King Arthur and the Knights of
the Round Table, are now chiefly inhabited by
market gardeners who supply London with its
fresh vegetables.

The palatial home of the Muses Club contains a pretty little theatre upon the toy stage
of which, as the American Friend and I entered, a lady of uncertain age, whose name,
given on the printed programme, was utterly
unknown to me, was singing a cheap street
ballad in a cracked voice.   I gave the American Friend a reproachful glance.   He only
laughed, and ordered a bottle of champagne.
The place was thick with the smoke of cigars.
Every one was in evening dress, and it was evi-

dent that the greater part of the audience was
familiar with the usages of good society. The
only concession to Bohemianism was the cigars
and the tables for refreshments. The Earl of
Drippingeaves bowed to me from the opposite
side of the theatre; but I pretended not to
recognize him. When the lady with the
cracked voice had been followed by a red-faced
gentleman with no voice at all, a monologuist
who could not remember his lines, and several
more of the most dismal failures to entertain I
had ever encountered, I turned to the American Friend with an indignant demand for an
explanation.

"Oh, this is merely preliminary," he said.
"This programme is specially arranged for the
nobodies."

"The nobodies?"

"Yes, for people whose applications for invitations cannot very well be refused, yet who
have no real claim on the Club's hospitality."

"Where do we come in?" I asked, anxiously.

"We are among the elect, my dear. Just be
patient for a few minutes longer."

The entertainment became more gruesome,
if possible, as it proceeded; but each number
was vigorously applauded by the "nobodies,"

who followed the example of prominent club members, that crafty example apparently convincing them of the error of their own judgment. When the ordeal was over the "nobodies" departed in high spirits, evidently under the impression that they had been bona fide guests of the Muses Club, and, accordingly, would be the envy ever afterward of their friends who had sought that honor in vain.

The President of the club, a successful librettist, who had maintained a solemn and pompous demeanor in the presence of the nobodies, became instantly transformed into a witty and most agreeable companion. He placed me under his personal protection, introducing me to several ladies and gentlemen occupying high positions on the stage and in the fields of art and literature, and finally leading the way to the supper-room, where a single long table was presently surrounded by a score of guests, all in evening dress, but all having shaken off the *noli me tangere* aspect which had rendered their presence so chilling in the theatre. When we sat down there were six or seven places still vacant. When the champagne corks had begun to pop one of the vacant places was quietly taken by a little man with a sharp, inquisitive nose, hollow cheeks, deep-set eyes, and a smile that illuminated his ugly face in a manner wonderful to behold. He was almost shabbily dressed in a rough sack suit. For a moment I wondered whether his presence would be tolerated. The next moment my wonder took an entirely different direction. The progress of the banquet was interrupted by what seemed to be a general determination to do the little plain man honor. The President left his seat and went over to shake the little man's hand warmly and begin an animated conversation with him. Others left their places and gathered about his chair. A celebrated actress playfully pushed macaroons into the little man's mouth so rapidly that he was unable to answer the witty questions she deluged him with.

" Who is the ragamuffin with the funny face?" I asked, addressing the American Friend.

" That is a London celebrity, my dear, whom you may only meet socially when you are yourself a specially honored guest of the Muses Club. Once the Duchess of Edgecombe sent her carriage for him. He sent back word that his time was worth a guinea a minute."

" If he told the truth," said I, " why doesn't he purchase himself a respectable suit of clothes?"

"He never thinks of clothes. There are good grounds to believe that he sleeps in those he has on."

"I believe it, at any rate. Look at his finger nails."

"He lives in his studio; he is a famous landscape painter."

"Has he never heard of soap?"

"He is too busy to think of soap."

"How sunken are his eyes and his cheeks."

"He sits up all night writing sonnets for the publishers, lyrics for opera librettists; his cheeks are sunken because he forgets to eat."

"What an expressive face he has."

"There is no better pantomimist in London."

"In spite of his ill-fitting clothes there is a grace about his movements that "—

"He is the best male dancer in London—a ballet master whose authority is never questioned by the managers who can afford to employ him."

"His speaking voice seems musical; you have only to add that he is the greatest tenor in Europe to bring me to his feet," said I.

"If Jean De Reszke had his marvelous power of expressing the utmost significance of the sentiment to which his music is set, the great

tenor would be incomparably greater than he
now is. This little man is absolute master of all
means of expression. Abstract ideals of beauty,
of which every imaginative mind is conscious,
find different forms of outward manifestation.
All these forms were known to savages. The
individual whose sense of sight is best developed
expresses his ideal of beauty with the pencil,
the brush or the chisel ; the imaginative person
whose sense of hearing is especially acute, and
whose mind is orderly, expresses his ideal in
the harmony of sounds ; and so throughout the
category of the senses. The possession of a
sensitive palate brings into being a great cook,
whom kings delight to honor. The cook's ideal
is, in the abstract, no less beautiful than that of
the painter or the composer. The abstract ideal
of beauty is universal. Occasionally it finds
universal expression. I have no doubt that the
plain little man over there has a palate as sensitive as that of the chef of the Savoy ; and that
if he is not already a great cook, it is simply
because he has not yet discovered his palate."

"Thank you," said I; "how extremely interesting. But, listen—something is going to
happen."

The little man had risen, and, surrounded by

an admiring group, was striking a series of attitudes for the enlightenment of the actress. The movements of his body seemed as intelligible as a spoken language. The actress clapped her hands.

"You are right, Geordie; you are always right." And she fed him with more macaroons.

"Good gracious!" I exclaimed; "she calls the great man, 'Geordie!'"

"So do all the elect at the Muses Club!" said the American Friend.

"Have you written anything more that is too good for the public, Geordie?" the actress was saying between macaroons.

"Nothing can be too good for the public," said the little man. "Some things good in conception lack artistic discretion in their execution. I believe I have in mind an instance or two, which I might"—

"Hear! Hear!" cried a dozen enthusiastic voices.

"Do you mean the things we had that dispute about in your studio day before yesterday?" asked the brilliant young composer who sat at the end of the table opposite the President.

"Yes," answered the little man; "but you

were mistaken. It depends on the interpretation. The words are nothing; the interpretation in voice and action is everything. Without proper interpretation the public will see only the author's indiscretion."

" Oh, come, now, Geordie. What do we care for the public here? Let the public go hang. Ladies and gentlemen, Geordie and I will now proceed to show you what the public misses, not owing to the sterility of our authors "—

" Hear! Hear!" said a trio of well-known song writers sitting in a bunch.

" But owing to the lamentable paucity of interpretative artists—present company of course excepted," added the composer, as the actress made a defiant face at him. " Ladies and gentlemen, Geordie will now interpret for you that monument of artistic indiscretion called ' The Interrupted Serenade.' "

Whereupon the composer took his seat at the piano and struck up a spirited Spanish martial air. Instantly the whole aspect of the little man was transformed. He seemed to become many inches taller. Pride of ancestry was in the glance of his haughty eye. No one saw his stained fingers, his shabby, ill-fitting clothes;

they saw only a Spanish Cavalier. Presently
the music, without loosing its character softened into a succession of chords which seemed
to invite declamation, and the Cavalier began
to recite the first verse of —

THE INTERRUPTED SERENADE

Don Cervantes Christobal
　Loved Inez of Seville,
And Inez loved Don Christobal,
　Yet snubbed him with a will.
For Christobal, in brave array,
　Each night his lute would bring,
And 'neath her window he would play
　And thus would try to sing:

Here the piano accompaniment flowed into
the familiar measures of a Spanish serenade,
the composer expertly imitating the twanging
of guitar strings. The attitude of the Cavalier
became that of a love-lorn swain standing beneath the window of his lady love. He struck
the strings of his imaginary lute, and, suddenly
twisting his countenance into an appropriate,
while extremely ludicrous, expression, sang the
refrain:

Oh, lul-lul-lul-lady fuf-fuf-fuf-fuf-fair,
　O-pup-pen thy window to me.
Huh-heavy with perfume the mum-midnight air,
　Fuf-full is mum-my heart of thee.

One gul-gul-gul-ance of thy bub-beauteous face
  My bosom with ju-joy would fill;
One sight of thy mum-mum-mum-mum-matchless grace
  With rapture mum-my soul would thrill.

The absurdity of the travesty, and the side-splitting manner in which it was interpreted, threw those about the table into convulsions of merriment. But the composer held up his hand in warning that the climax had not yet been reached, and Geordie began the recitation of the other verse:

Inez of Seville at length
  Bethought her of a plan
To stop these stutt'ring serenades,
  And to her window ran.
"I'll mix reproof with compliment,"
  She said, and then she sighed—
She loved the Knight, you understand—
  Then threw the lattice wide:

Now the little man underwent another transformation. He was no longer the Spanish Cavalier, nor the stuttering serenader; but Inez of Seville looking down from her casement and singing mischievously:

Oh, dud-dud-dud-dud-dud-dud-Don Christobal,
  O-pup-pen thine ears to mum-me.
Why sus-sus-sus-sing at tut-tut-tut-all?
  Dud-dancing's much better for thee.

Your tut-tut-tut-tongue it is tut-tut-tut-tied,
   Your lul-lul-lul-legs are a dream ;
Just dud-dud-dud-dance for thine Inez awhile,
   And sus-sus-sus-see how it will seem!

Paying no attention to the shrieks of laughter from those who surrounded the supper table, the little man broke into a wild dance with pantomimic adjuncts, in which he was presently joined by the actress. Together, while the composer continued to officiate in perfect sympathy at the piano, they represented, with burlesque variations, most of the music-hall specialties at that time popular. In spite of his extraordinary exertions the little man showed absolutely no evidence of fatigue. The only interruption of his novel and varied performance was when the actress insisted on feeding him ice cream with a large spoon in order to demonstrate that "Geordie's mouth was built on the same patent collapsable, elastic, generally adaptable, plan that distinguished his recent invention of Universal Christmas Pantomime Scenery." Upon the successful conclusion of this demonstration, the composer, who had taken upon himself the office of master of ceremonies, rapped for order and said:

"Geordie will now give an imitation of a

timid young man dining *tête-à-tête* with a pretty
girl who expects to be kissed after dessert."

"Hear! Hear!" I found myself saying with
the others.

The little man placed a single chair at a little
distance from the piano, from which the composer had begun to extract a programme of
second-class table d'hote music. Then, with a
startled look accompanied by many evidences
of extreme nervousness, he appeared to enter
from the street with a lady, which imaginary
person he seated in an imaginary chair which
he pushed up carefully to an imaginary table,
and then seated himself opposite to her in the
real chair already mentioned. No further description is necessary to indicate the manner in
which this extraordinary person, half singing,
half reciting, illuminated the two verses of the
song called:

PIT-A-PAT I PALPITATE

Whene'er Chlorinda dines with me
    At Signor Tonti's table d'hote,
From soup to coffee dimples she
    Coy meanings which I, trembling, note;
For when the menu pleases her,
    (Which Tonti's rarely fails to do)
My woes her soft emotions stir—

And then's the time for me to woo!
Alas! uncertain of my fate,
  Pit-a-pat I palpitate!
The consommé cools on my plate—
  Pit-a-pit I palpitate!
I tremble lest I am too late,
I'm in a very nervous state —
  Pit-a-pat I palpitate!
  Pit-a-pat I palpitate!

The band's sweet strains fall on my heart
  As though to spur my lagging zeal;
Chlorinda's red lips gently part,
  Her bosom heaves in mute appeal.
Yet I for courage pray in vain,
  Nor can my scattered wits arrange;
The waiter comes and goes again —
  I pay the bill, he keeps the change.
Alas! Alack! my doleful fate!
  Pit-a-apat I palpitate!
Chlorinda's brows are dark with hate —
  Pit-a-pat I palpitate!
Oh, now I know I am too late.
I'm in a very wretched state —
  Pit-a-pat I palpitate!
  Pit-a-pat I palpitate!

As may be imagined, our party was now in a very merry mood verging closely on the hilarious. Several of those about the table had been crowned by their companions with wreaths twined from the handsome floral decorations. Geordie's genius suddenly took a classical turn.

Dexterously draping his lean figure in a table cloth he began posing as a Vestal Virgin.

"Silence!" commanded the master of cere-monies. "We will now have something emi-nently worthy of the occasion. All those wear-ing wreaths will form over here by the piano for the chorus. Geordie will now relate how the Ionian Maid explained—ahem—to the— er—to the proper authorities how she came to lose—ahem—to lose something which she could never hope to regain."

"Hear! Hear!" cried everybody, while the chorus formed as directed, the composer struck some chords of appropriate sylvan simplicity, and the little man proceeded to interpret with the assistance of the chorus:

THE IONIAN MAID'S EXCUSE

Love took me by the hand one day
  And led me o'er the flowery plain ;
Oh, merry as a child at play,
  He laughed, nor thought of age nor pain.
Love, youth and Maytime!
  Over the flow'ry meads we go.
Ah, then is playtime —
  Youth, love and flowers will have it so!

Love laughed away my prudent fears ;
  He crowned me with a wreath of flowers;
He said that age was time for tears,
  And bade me laugh while youth was ours.

Love, youth and Maytime !
Over the flow'ry meads we go.
Ah, then is playtime —
Love, youth and flowers will have it so!

Finally every one present, save the American
Friend and myself, joined in the refrain of this
somewhat suggestive ditty, forming with the
chorus and accompanying their singing with
classical Greek poses which were, of course,
perfectly dignified and decorous.

This was deemed an appropriate conclusion of
the ceremony of the " Unbending of the Wits,"
as the American Friend termed it. A few minutes later we were all departing, after I had received the most cordial assurances that "London
was not at all a stupid place when you come to
penetrate beneath the surface." I felt that I
could heartily endorse the sentiment.

CHAPTER XV

ONE night a little more than a week after Tommy Atkins' rash acceptance of Captain Lively's invitation to a late supper at Hyde Park Barracks, I noticed that presistent person sitting in a front stall bending upon myself and my understudy—Tommy appearing now in the small part which utilized her talents ordinarily—looks of settled gloom, in which it seemed to me there was a suggestion of menace. Had the Captain discovered his error? Was he able at last to distinguish between the genuine article and its imitation? Was he aware that he had been lavishing upon the understudy attentions intended for the prima donna? If so, what did he purpose doing about it? I felt that I, as well as Tommy, could await the sequel with equanimity. What could Captain Lively consistently, and with dignity becoming his station, do but keep his own council?

But I had not at that time acquired the large

knowledge respecting the typical British male character which I now possess. A brief digression will enable me to prepare the mind of my American readers to receive with entire confidence the plain statement I am about to make of Captain Lively's subsequent behavior.

There is no greater fallacy than that which pictures the average Englishman as a reckless spendthrift. My countrymen are too apt to form their judgment upon the conduct of the exceptions—upon the dissipated noblemen who squander their substance in usurious interest paid to Jew money lenders, upon men at the head of their professions who ruin themselves at the gaming tables of Monte Carlo, and upon those Napoleons of finance who sink brilliantly in the maelstrom of their own collapsed enterprises. These are exceptions, and exceedingly rare ones at that. The average Englishman is a monument of practical sense and conduct. If he sees that you are a gentleman—according to the English standard which prescribes that your pocket always contains a sovereign or two wherewith to meet promptly the small obligations which constantly stare a gentleman in the face in London, not to speak of the nimble shilling with which to tip the British servitor—he

will invite you to his club, to his town and his
country house, and will entertain you lavishly.
But if you should find yourself short of funds,
even temporarily, do not dream of confessing it
even in a whisper to yourself. Steal silently
away on your last shilling. To request of him
the temporary loan of ten pounds would be
fatal. The temperature of the Klondike in
January is balmy to that with which he would
be instantly enveloped. And he will never
thaw to you again.

Don't believe the stories of those who declare
that Englishmen are reckless investors. They
are gamblers, but they gamble only according
to their means. The national family idol of
England is the Fixed Income. Except among
the laboring and the poorest classes even the
children have fixed incomes. This is the system: We will say that the head of a family, a
country property-holder, has a rent roll which
foots up twenty thousand pounds annually.
One half of this is required to maintain the
family and meet the permanent charges of the
estate. Half of the remainder will be invested
safely, say in British consols, or in real estate,
the compounding of the resulting income year
after year forming usually funds for other spe-

cific investments which are made in the names
of the young members of the family, who, as
they become old enough to appreciate the ad-
vantages of an independent income, however
small, are initiated into the mysteries of the
system and proceed to draw their own checks
to meet their personal expenses. As they grow
older and these expenses increase their princi-
pals are augmented by legacies left them by
relatives, which are one of the delightful and
inevitable consequences of the operation of this
system. And so, from generation to generation, the ball keeps rolling. Every member of
the family, uncles, aunts, cousins, down to the
poorest relation, has a fixed income, big or little, and enjoys the esteem of British society
accordingly.

In our financial scheme it will be observed
that we have left an annual surplus of five
thousand pounds. Having met, as we have
seen, all the fixed obligations of his system, the
head of the family regards this surplus from
the standpoint of the prudent gambler. In its
absence American promoters and English Napoleons of finance would perish of starvation in
London, and the gaming tables of Monte Carlo
would not know the color of British gold. The

possessor of these five thousand pounds is willing to risk them on any enterprise that holds forth reasonable inducements of large gain. He hopes to win, but he is prepared to lose. He usually loses, of course. But he can afford to, and that is the reason why American promoters continue to live in the best hotels in the British metropolis.

Practically all English army officers are beneficiaries of the system I have described—a fact which will tend further to give credence to the revelations respecting Captain Lively and Tommy Atkins with which Prue regaled me while I was dressing for the second act.

Prue seemed preoccupied. She laid out the wrong stockings, and she pricked me twice while repairing a rent in my bodice.

"Prue," I said, finally. "You have something on your mind."

"I have, indeed." And she sighed.

"Is the rent due again?" I asked, with trepidation.

"The rent is paid a month in advance." And she sighed again.

"Prue, you are homesick."

"And you," retorted Prue, "are as blind as a bat."

"Surely you don't mean," I began in alarm, "that Daffy and the Liar "—

"That pair of idiots, bah!" interrupted my companion with an expression of supreme disdain. "No, I don't even mean Miss Casino and Lord Dangerford "—

"Countess Pipedreme and Lord Dangerford, is you please," I interrupted in my turn. "Have you already forgotten the little comedy at the Ascot races of which I told you?"

"And you have forgotten the quarrel between Lord Dangerford and Captain Lively at the Pall Mall Club, which was more than hinted at in yesterday's *Gazette?*" said Prue.

"Not guilty, Prue," I answered, laughing. "Tommy Atkins, not I, was the *casus belli* You know that as well as I do."

"And you know," croaked Prue, "that Tommy Atkins doesn't enter into the matter at all except as your double. Trouble is coming out of it, mark my word. That English upstart in the chorus—Sloppy Weather—has been stirring it up for a week past."

"Sloppy Weather," I laughed. "Isn't she the absurd creature who is fined regularly each week for her slipshod way of dressing?"

"She deserves it, too."

"She always makes the same comment when she opens her envelope and finds her salary seven shillings short: 'I consider the conduct of the manager most undignified.' Is that the girl, Prue?"

"That's the girl. Haven't you noticed how popular she has suddenly become with the other girls in the company?"

"No; is that possible?"

"And how they are all giving Tommy Atkins the cold shoulder?"

"No, I hadn't observed it."

Prue heaved a third sigh, longer drawn and more ominous than either of the others.

"Well, Prue?"

"It's all on account of Tommy's diamonds," snapped my companion.

"You don't mean that Tommy Atkins is wearing diamonds? You can't mean Tommy Atkins, Prue?" It was my turn to become agitated.

"She's covered with them."

"Prue," I said with energy, "don't you go about croaking and shaking your head on Tommy Atkins' account. Tommy's all right."

"She wears diamonds worth a thousand

pounds. Hardly a girl in the company has spoken to her for a week."

"They are jealous," said I.

"She rides in Rotten Row every morning with Captain Lively."

"That's Tommy's own affair, Prue."

"Daffy says she saw her driving in Hyde Park in a brougham."

"Well, what of that, so long as it isn't Tommy's brougham?"

"Who says it isn't Tommy's brougham?" croaked Prue.

"I do," I replied, stoutly.

"You said the same thing about Totsy Wenn, who drove to the theatre in a brougham on the third night after our opening, who left the company the next day, and who, if half the stories about her may be believed, is mistress of one of the handsomest apartments in the West End."

"Prue," said I, "once for all let me tell you that Totsy Wenn and Tommy Atkins are two persons. They are no more alike than night is like day."

Prue hesitated a moment and then said:

"Of course that may be all a mistake about Tommy Atkins' flat in Victoria Street."

" Three of her former bosom friends."—Page 211

"Who is responsible for that calumny?" I demanded.

"Sloppy Weather didn't exactly say it; but she hinted it."

"Sloppy Weather will do well to be a little careful about her hints. Tommy Atkins lives in an ordinary boarding-house in Gower Street."

"Are you sure?"

"Absolutely. I called on her there this afternoon."

During the progress of the second act I had an opportunity to verify Prue's remark about Tommy's diamonds, and also about the chilly attitude toward her maintained by most of the girls in the chorus. A diamond pendant of dazzling brillancy nestled in the hollow of Tommy's pretty throat; at least half a dozen diamonds, a handsome ruby and an emerald or two blazed on her fingers. She seemed to be in a very pleasant frame of mind. Once when her back was turned toward the audience I saw her laugh and snap her fingers in the faces of Sloppy Weather and three of her former bosom friends. In his stall just beyond the footlights Captain Lively still sat plunged in his gloomy reflections.

The storm suddenly broke while I was changing for the third act. Little Bobby, looking pale and startled, thrust her head into my dressing-room and said:

"Come as quickly as you can. Tommy Atkins has been arrested."

"Tommy?—Arrested?"

Little Bobby, breathless, nodded. "She's a prisoner in her dressing-room. She says you can clear her."

"Say that I will come immediately. Prue, hurry up with my third act dress."

Two minutes later I was admitted to Tommy's room. It was a large room shared with three other girls, who had received hasty instructions from the stage manager to vacate the premises. This functionary, wearing a belligerent look, was in the midst of a sarcastic argument with a bailiff, while a dingy gentleman in black with a long sallow face and a red nose, holding a silk hat in his hand, kept repeating:

"Be careful, my dear sir. Do be careful I beg of you. Under our laws language is actionable no less than the overt act. Restrain yourself, I beg of you."

Tommy Atkins, perfectly composed, sat staring quizzically at the court officer and the dingy gentleman.

"What is the meaning of this?" I demanded in my most indignant tones.

"Gently, softly, my dear young lady," began the dingy gentleman; "everything can be arranged, I assure you."

"And who may you be, sir?" I asked.

"Waxem—Fletcher Q. Waxem, madam; four seventy Temple Chambers; plaintiff's attorney in the case of Captain Gerald Lively against Caroline Clarke, alias Tommy Atkins, for obtaining valuable jewels under false pretenses."

"Not guilty," said Tommy with emphasis.

"Certainly not," said I.

"Very good; very good indeed," said Mr. Waxem, with a professional smile of approval. "Unfortunately, however, witnesses here present are prepared to identify property and swear to finding same in possession and on the person of defendant. Would state that it is in my discretion, on surrender of property, to suppress service of warrant."

"Do you mean," said I, "that if Tommy Atkins gives up the diamonds"—

"I won't give up the diamonds," said Tommy, in a cool, hard voice.

"Certainly she won't give up the diamonds," said the stage manager, adding a few native

American expletives which caused Mr. Waxem to hold up his warning finger again.

"Certainly we will not give up the diamonds," said I. "Your accusation is rubbish. Do your worst."

Mr. Waxem looked disappointed. "Very serious charge," he said, casting a solemn look in Tommy's direction. "Evidence conclusive. Sentence of the court in all probability transportation."

"Rubbish!" exclaimed Tommy. "You tell your precious client to meet me in the Police Court to-morrow morning. I'll make him look like tuppence ha'penny. I'm ready, Officer." And Tommy, throwing a long cloak over her stage costume, exhibited her willingness to depart at once.

The lawyer threw open the door and motioned to the officer. I thought at the time that he was bluffing and later developments proved that I was not mistaken.

"Don't you be so keen," said the officer, sullenly; "I ain't satisfied about this 'ere case."

"You didn't issue the warrant," sneered the attorney.

"But it's in my discretion to serve it or tear it up," retorted the bailiff.

"You'd better not let your discretion run away with you. Defendant admits she's not Miss Casino."

"What of that?" demanded Tommy, throwing off her cloak.

"Statement's equivalent to admission of false pretenses," said the dingy man.

"Rubbish," said Tommy.

The door had been left open. Little Bobby, the Comédienne, Daffy, and Sloppy Weather had entered, and half a dozen chorus girls' anxious faces looked in over their shoulders. The bailiff glanced again at the warrant which he held in his hand, reflected a moment, and said to Tommy:

"I don't want to serve this 'ere paper. It's a serious matter and would make you a lot of trouble whichever way the case went. My advice is that you give up the diamonds to Captain Lively's attorney."

"Never," said Tommy with angry emphasis. Then turning to the group in the door, she said:

"Girls, did any of you ever see me wear a diamond until a week ago?"

"No," said Little Bobby. The others shook their heads.

"You never had the chance," said Sloppy
Weather, spitefully.

"Shut up, you cat," said Daffy, turning sav-
agely on the English girl. Plainly the tide of
public opinion back of the scenes was turning
in Tommy's favor.

"I consider your language most undignified,"
said Sloppy Weather.

To the manifest alarm of the attorney,
Tommy Atkins was removing the diamonds
from her neck and her fingers. Presently,
holding the glittering heap in her hand, she
said:

"Girls, I care nothing for such trinkets. I
never did. All I care about now is teaching
Captain Lively a lesson that he'll remember—a
lesson that all his dissipated companions will
hear of and take to heart. Girls, do I need to
explain to you the base motive which prompted
Captain Gerald Lively, of Her Majesty's Life
Guards, to give me these diamonds?"

"No!" screamed a chorus of angry voices.

"Do you believe me when I declare on my
honor that I accepted them without any sacrifice of my self-respect?"

"Yes!"

"Captain Lively's demand for the return of the jewels proves that, my dear," said I.

"Thank you," said Tommy, and I saw that there were tears in her eyes. Then turning to the attorney she said:

"You may report to your client that I not only refuse to give up the diamonds, but that I have distributed them among my personal friends in the company as souvenirs of one victory over our common enemy."

Tommy held up the diamond pendant and smiled at me:

"Will you take this, dear?"

"No, my dear," said I. "You forget that I am your accomplice."

"You'll take it, won't you, dear?" Tommy offered the jewel to the Comédienne.

"Indeed I will, you darling!"

The two girls fell into each other's arms. As the glittering bauble changed hands the dingy man began dancing up and down in his excitement.

"Officer," he fairly screamed, "you are my witness. The defendant is disposing of the stolen property"—

"Sir!" said Tommy, sternly. "Stolen? Repeat that if you please!"

Whereupon she began distributing the rings. The attorney, now frantic, produced a note-book and scribbled away for dear life:

"The diamond pendant to girl known as the Comédienne; medium height, with dark hair and eyes. Keep your eyes open, Officer! Ring set with two large diamonds to girl known as Little Bobby; curly hair and brown eyes. Make a note of it, Officer! Ring set with rubies to girl known as Daffy; tall with haughty expression. Make a note of it, Officer; you are my witness." And so on until the last diamond had been given away.

"Aren't you going to keep one for yourself, dear?" said I.

"I need no souvenir," replied Tommy; "I've had the experience."

"Officer," said the dingy man, panting with anger and the effects of his exertions, "I really think we are justified in placing all these ladies under arrest."

"Gammon!" exclaimed the bailiff, bending upon Tommy a glance of sincere admiration.

"False pretenses admitted, disposal of property in question aggravates offence," said the attorney.

"There were no false pretenses," said I.

"Certainly not," assented Tommy.

"What!" screamed the dingy man."

"I told Captain Lively in Miss Casino's presence that I was not the person he had called to
see," said Tommy.

"I told Captain Lively in Tommy Atkins'
presence that I was Miss Casino, the person he
had called to see; but he would not believe it,"
said I.

"Ah-a, a witness! a witness!" screamed the
dingy man, the perspiration rolling down his
face.

I saw Prue's face in the doorway.

"Prue," said I, "tell this gentleman what
you know about it."

"On the night that Captain Lively forced
his way upon the stage, and to the door of Miss
Casino's dressing-room," said Prue, with evident
enjoyment, "Tommy Atkins was preparing to
go on as Miss Casino's understudy. In spite
of their explanations Captain Lively insisted
upon extending his invitation to Tommy. I
was in the room all the time. Miss Casino
even followed them to the Captain's carriage,
still assuring him of his mistake; but he paid
no attention to her."

"Drop it?" said the officer to the attorney, pocketing his warrant.

The dingy man was showing his teeth. He turned to Tommy.

"On what grounds do you claim the diamonds?"

"On the ground that they were presented to me by Captain Lively."

"What return did you make to Captain Lively for his—er—his extreme generosity?"

"My society," said Tommy; "my society three times at supper after the performance, five mornings and four afternoons in Hyde Park, and one Sunday on the Thames to Windsor and back."

"Don't you think that your society comes rather high at a thousand pounds' worth of diamonds and rubies?"

"Not when Captain Gerald Lively is the other party," retorted Tommy.

"Drop it! look 'ere now, Waxem, you drop it," said the bailiff.

"Hold on," said the attorney, triumphantly, "there's another charge. How about drawing a deadly weapon on Her Majesty's uniform at Hyde Park Barracks on the—let me see "—the attorney consulted his note-book—"on the nine-

teenth day of May, Anno Domini, eighteen hundred and ninety-eight? How about drawing a
deadly weapon on Captain Lively, Miss—Miss
Tommy Atkins?"

Tommy's face was scarlet. But she held her
head high and answered:

"Girls, you will understand. Captain Lively
was intoxicated. . . . It was after supper.
I found myself suddenly alone with him. . . .
When I sought to leave the place I discovered
that the door was locked. . . . Captain
Lively was in no condition to listen to reason. . . . I was at his mercy. . . . At
the last moment I did the only thing left for
me to do. I drew this." And like a flash
Tommy whipped from its mysterious place of
concealment the terribly business-like revolver
with which she had illustrated for me her Montana experiences.

"Drop it!" growled the bailiff.

The dingy man gasped once or twice, threw
a venomous look about the circle of derisive
faces, and silently departed, the bailiff following at his heels.

A minute later the curtain rose on the third
act. Captain Lively had evidently heard his
emissary's report. His stall was empty.

CHAPTER XVI

LADY Slasher turned her fine eyes full upon my own. A lovely smile illuminated her kind face, too often saddened by the expression that mirrored her almost constant reflections upon the social prejudices which dwarf the souls and bodies of humanity. She seized both my hands and said in her impulsive way:

"Oh, my dear, how your words thrill me!"

"They are the expression of thoughts that thrill me," I answered.

"Keep on having such thoughts," said Lady Slasher with enthusiasm. "Keep on expressing them. The thought and its expression strengthen the will. The human will, when fully impressed upon the consciousness of its possessor, is as nearly omnipotent as anything this side of Heaven. Do you not remember what Balzac says about the will? Ah, that splendid intellect! He refuses to limit its powers to the spiritual side of man which gave it birth. He boldly declares the will to be a material force. My dear, only think of it. You will to shatter stone battlements and forthwith they crumble into dust!"

"But how long it must take to develop one's will to a point where it is strong enough to accomplish anything," I said, feeling lamentably weak in the presence of this remarkable woman.

"You must give it practice—daily practice on the small obstructions first," said Lady Slasher. "Your will gained in power a hundred fold when you poured those ardently patriotic words into the ear of the Marquis of Silsbury which inspired His Lordship to make the significant comment which you just now repeated to me. Remember that the next time you meet His Lordship. His will in that matter, if not already secretly coincident with your own, is at least passive. It is a field made ready for your sowing. Seed time is as at hand, my dear."

"But how can we wait for the harvest?" I exclaimed. "When you, a weak young girl like myself, in your American home, looked at the plump, sleek, perfect bodies of the little pigs in your father's barnyard, you know that it would be years and years before you could prevail upon men and women to give the same attention to the development and perpetuation of their own species that every one who has pigs gives to the future of their Berkshires and their Poland Chinas. You knew that your mission would require years, perhaps generations for its accomplishment; mine must be accomplished immediately. Already the Powers—England alone excepted—are secretly offering their ships to Spain."

Lady Slasher smiled encouragingly. "The opportunity finds the man, why not the woman? My dear, I fully believe that in this emergency you are the woman, and that the opportunity is at hand. You shall help me receive this afternoon. I can hardly hope for so much honor as the presence of the Marquis of Silsbury—but wait, and do not be impatient."

In response to Lady Slasher's urgent request I had arrived an hour earlier than the time named in the invitations to her "Anglo-American Garden Party," to which all London was bidden. Her brilliant marriage to a British Peer had by no means obliterated Lady Slasher's affection for the land of her birth—no more than it had slackened in the slightest degree her zeal in the great cause which has made her lectures and her books famous throughout America and Europe. Never during the early years of her journalistic slavery in America had she toiled

more persistently for the overthrow of the fe-
tishes of society than she now toiled in her
English country palace convenient to London,
surrounded by every luxury that a woman of
leisure and refinement could desire. She entertained lavishly, but it was perfectly understood that she never accepted invitations in return for her own hospitality. Naturally her
extreme views on social subjects caused her to
be looked at askance by the prudes of society,
and by those who feel themselves lost except
when anchored fast to the rock of convention-
ality. It was only the knowledge that there
was no danger of Lady Slasher ever setting her
iconoclastic feet upon their own hearth stones
that emboldened such persons to visit her at
all. This situation was already so familiar to
me that I felt confident of meeting at Lady
Slasher's garden party many of the finest folk
in England—her wine cellars were known to be
inexhaustible.

Lady Slasher's grounds were magnificent.
Besides the natural shade furnished by fine
old spreading oaks there were canvas shelters
gayly decked out with red, white and blue
bunting and innumerable flags of the sister
nations. Tables were spread everywhere, and

there was no lack of comfortable seats, and snug little retreats among the shrubbery which seemed to have been provided for the special encouragement of love-making. Toward the middle of the afternoon, when my duty at Lady Slasher's side in helping to receive the guests had been fulfilled, I made a tour of the grounds, accompanied by the American Friend, and found every one of these retreats occupied. One of Lady Slasher's special recommendations to young men and women was her avowed sympathy with lovers. But I fear that on that afternoon many a desperate flirtation was born later to abuse her beneficence.

One of the surprises the afternoon brought me was my unexpected encounter with Countess Pipedreme and the Earl of Drippingeaves conversing earnestly in one of the shady nooks I have described. The Countess' conduct on observing my presence was no less surprising.

"In such a cause my purse is certainly at your disposal," she said, putting her handkerchief to her eyes. "Poor woman, how I pity her!"

Whereupon the Countess gave the Earl her hand and they separated.

"Angel of mercy," commented the American Friend with sarcasm.

"The idea of the Earl of Drippingeaves bothering his empty head about the sorrows of the poor," said I.

The incident was speedily driven from our minds by a spectacle of superior interest which confronted us as we moved toward the large oak near the centre of the grounds which served as a sort of sylvan audience chamber wherein the Queen of the ceremonies dispensed wisdom to all comers. The group which surrounded Lady Slasher exhibited signs of animation rather unusual in such a gathering. True to her instinct as a publicist, Lady Slasher had locked horns in an argument with Mr. Squibs of the *Gazette*. The Honorable Mrs. Pebblestone, Lady Dunstable and the Duchess of Edgecombe were in the front rank of interested listeners. I think I have already mentioned that Mr. Squibs enjoyed a social position rather unique among journalists, excepting, of course, the prominent critics, and the wealthy publishers whose consistent defence of the institution of royalty has been rewarded by their admission to that borderland of aristocracy, knighthood.

Knowing the quality of Mr. Squibs' wit we hastened to join the group.

"My dear," whispered Lady Dunstable, "it's almost shocking, of course, but so interesting."

"Between the pigs and the babies," Mr. Squibs was saying, "I admit that the pigs have the better start. But think of their tragic end!"

"You are begging the question," retorted Lady Slasher. "My comparison was limited to the fundamental proposition of birth. Birth is something that is thrust upon every living thing. The being that profits or is victimized by the fact of birth has no voice in the matter. The human victim, who, being endowed with intelligence, will live to appreciate the injustice heaped upon him, perhaps to curse those who selfishly brought this misery upon him. The pig, on the contrary, remains unconscious of his ideal entrance to life. Think of the brutal inequality of it! Human beings, created in the image of God, the only living creatures that are denied the advantage of a wholesome and natural parentage!"

Mr. Squibs threw up his hands with a comical gesture. "I give it up. I withdraw my babies from the argument. The little pigs have it."

"How highly improper," whispered the Honorable Mrs. Pebblestone to me as she moved eagerly a step or two nearer the disputants.

"But what are you going to have done about it?" Mr. Squibs demanded.

"That's it, you know," drawled the Earl of Drippingeaves. "The little babies can't pick out their own papas and mammas, don't you know, haw, haw, haw."

"I couldn't," said Mr. Squibs. "That's the reason I'm not a Duke."

"What nonsense," said Countess Pipedreme, haughtily. She had captured Lord Dangerford somewhere in the grounds and glued herself to his side.

"Countess Pipedreme has a right to be supercilious," whispered the American Friend in my ear, "being probably the only exception present to the rule just laid down."

"How can that be?" I asked, innocently.

"Haven't you heard how she happens to be a Countess?"

"No. I thought the mystery had never been explained."

"It never has been until this moment. You see she selected her own parents. That action having been postponed until she had gained considerable worldly wisdom, she took pains to select a Count for a father."

" Oh," I laughed, " that is what Teddy meant when, in answer to my inquiry about the origin of the title of Countess Pipedreme, he replied that she had dreamt it."

But Lady Slasher had not been in the slightest degree ruffled by the pleasantries of Mr. Squibs and the Earl of Drippingeaves. She smiled benevolently upon them and said:

" The remedy is very simple. The mothers of the future hold it in their hands."

" The male, not the female, is the race," quoted Mr. Squibs, triumphantly.

" Granted," was Lady Slasher's instant reply. " If it is a race of drunkards, of imbeciles, of degenerates, of physical wrecks, its blood be upon the head of the father."

" Oh, by all means, bar the drunken, degenerate, imbecile males, but how ? " demanded the journalist.

Lady Slasher fixed her brilliant eyes upon the sympathetic countenance of the Duchess of Edgecombe. " By educating liberally the temperate, wholesome-minded, clean-lived females," she said, with conviction in her tones.

"Children cannot select their parents, but the mothers may select the fathers."

"Oh! Ah! Dear me! The very idea!" Lady Slasher stood serene and smiling under the storm of exclamations which the group hurled upon her.

"I repeat," she said, "that the female should be allowed to select her mate."

"Oh, come now, you wouldn't have the women do the proposing?" said the Earl of Drippingeaves, aghast.

"Why not? She would never, of her own free will, select a drunkard or a libertine to be the father of her children. Under the present system she accepts them because she is ignorant, or because they are thrust upon her."

"You can never educate 'em up to it," said Mr. Squibs, shaking his head violently. "The dear creatures have been pursued since the very beginning, and they like it."

"It is ignorance," said Lady Slasher.

"It is gallantry," said Mr. Squibs. "What would our poetry be without it?"

"Superstition, superstition, superstition," retorted Lady Slasher. "Why did Rochefoucault say: 'Marriage is sometimes convenient, but never delightful'? Because so many women

are led so unwillingly to the altar. Marriages
engineered by men, dominated by the blind
passion of the moment, are not well assorted. I
will quote to you Lady Mary Wortley Motagu,
daughter of a Duke, beautiful, accomplished,
clear-headed, fashionable, in reply to Rochefoucault: 'It is impossible to taste the delights
of love in perfection but in a well assorted marriage. A fond couple attached to each other
by mutual affection, are two lovers who live hap-
pily together. Though the priest pronounces
certain words, though the lawyers draw up certain instruments, yet I look on these prepara-
tives in the same light as a lover considers a
rope ladder which he fastens to his mistress'
window: If they can but live together, what
does it signify by what means the union is accomplished? . . . When a pair who entertain such rational sentiments are united by in-
dissoluble bonds, all nature smiles upon them.
. . . In my opinion such a life is infinitely
more happy and more voluptuous than the most
ravishing and best regulated gallantry.'"

"When the daughter of a Duke says a thing,"
said Mr. Squibs, solemnly, "it is indeed time to
pause and reflect."

"But," objected the Earl of Drippingeaves,

"how does it help the matter to have women do the proposing?"

"Why, that's simple enough," said Mr. Squibs. "Women are so keen. A woman will have sense enough to select a husband whom she can fool into believing as long as he can stand on his pegs that he is perpetually climbing into her window by way of a rope ladder. We're such blooming idiots, you know, when we're well managed—by a woman."

"Still, I don't see where the blessed babies come in," objected the Earl.

"Really, how indelicate," murmured Lady Dunstable, putting her hand behind her ear.

Lady Slasher quoted from one of her famous essays: "Women are growing wiser. . . . Rakes and profligates of all descriptions they will reject. They will refuse to join themselves to any unless sound in body, mind and morals."

"I say, you're very dense, My Lord," said Mr. Squibs, turning to the Earl of Dripping-eaves. "When women do the proposing the Millennium will have arrived; in the Millennium the little pigs and the babies will start at the post neck and neck."

"Bravo! Hear, hear!" said a voice on the outskirts of the group which I seemed to recognize. I turned and my heart leaped into my throat. It was the Marquis of Silsbury, and on his arm leaned the Prince.

I could not at first believe the evidence of my eyes, it seemed so highly improbable that the Prince of Wales would confer upon Lady Slasher an honor which so many who represented the nobility in their own right had been denied. Then I reflected that this was to all intents and purposes a public gathering. More than two thousand persons were in the grounds —an assemblage hardly less democratic than that of which I had been a member at the Ascot races. There was a great stir immediately, but I noticed that the assemblage maintained strictly its public character. No one save his intimate friends spoke to the Prince. His Royal Highness, after being welcomed by Lady Slasher, spoke a few words with her, and then walked about the grounds with the Duchess of Edgecombe, the crowd keeping at a respectful distance.

" Oh, if I could only meet him ! " I said.

" Who, the Prince ? " asked the American Friend.

" Oh, no ; of course I don't expect that. I mean the Marquis of Silsbury. You haven't

forgotten what he said that night at the chop
house where we met the man who knew
Dickens?"

"Hardly. By the way, it does look as
though now is your time"—

"Look!" I exclaimed. "He recognizes
you; he is bowing."

The American Friend returned the Marquis
of Silsbury's pleasant salutation, remarking to
me: "He hasn't forgotten you, either. See,
he is coming this way."

It was true. The Marquis had started in
our direction; but Countess Pipedreme, inspired by her unaccountable animosity toward
me, seemed to divine His Lordship's intention.
She dragged Lord Dangerford across the
Marquis' path, accosting him gayly in a manner
which left a gallant man no choice but to listen
to her. I was delighted to notice, however,
that His Lordship was not to be balked of his
purpose.

"Come," said the American Friend, giving
me a sly look, "we will meet him half way."

"No, no," I said, feeling that something un-
pleasant was about to happen. "It will em-
barrass Lord Dangerford. I never saw him so
agitated."

"What has he to be agitated about? There is no reason why he should not present you to the Marquis. The Duchess of Edgecombe has received you. Lady Dunstable is your avowed friend—what the deuce!"

The Countess had raised her shrill voice and was saying: "You meet them everywhere, these stage women, My Lord. There's no keeping them in their place."

They were right upon us. Lord Dangerford's face crimsoned with anger. He cast a look of contempt upon the Countess, then taking off his hat and bowing, he said:

"My Lord, permit me to present a most estimable young lady,"—

"Arthur!" exclaimed Countess Pipedreme, stamping her foot with rage.

"Whom I respect highly," went on His Lordship, ignoring the Countess' violent protest, "Miss Casino."

"Go to your mistress, then," hissed the Countess, her face livid as she stared at me insolently and drew her skirts about her. "At least be honest with the Marquis of Silsbury —your mistress"—

"Countess," said Lord Dangerford, huskily, "you forget yourself."

The Earl of Drippingeaves was passing.

" My Lord," said Countess Pipedreme, " will you give me your arm? "

The Earl gave Lord Dangerford a startled glance, offered his arm sheepishly to the Countess who, shrugging her shoulders disdainfully, led her new victim to a distant part of the grounds.

CHAPTER XVII

FOR a single moment I wished that the earth might open and bury me forever. I felt myself swaying, felt the American Friend's grasp on my arm tighten, while in the distance I seemed to hear some one saying how glad he was to make my acquaintance. I was not sure that this sentiment proceeded from the Marquis of Silsbury until I found him bending gallantly above my hand, which he touched to his lips with charming old-fashioned grace.

Lord Dangerford was smiling, but very pale. With the most admirable tact and delicacy these kind-hearted gentlemen—true noblemen, both—gave me not a moment for reflection.

"Bless me, but I haven't felt so peckish in a long time," said the Marquis. "That salad over there fairly hypnotizes me."

"Lady Slasher's champagne is not to be despised, either," said Lord Dangerford. "I don't see why we should allow it to be wasted altogether on a mob like this."

238

So they laughingly urged me toward one of the large refreshment tables. On the way we picked up the Honorable Mrs. Pebblestone, while the American Friend wandered off to do missionary work among some newly arrived inhabitants of the United States who had not yet conquered their surprise at the strange customs of the natives.

Soon the Marquis and I were chattering away as though we had known each other for years, with Lord Dangerford and the Honorable Mrs. Pebblestone chiming in here and there with a laughing comment. I burned to broach the subject that was next my heart. Lady Slasher was smiling upon me from a distance, and nodding significantly. But I had a presentiment that something was shortly to happen that would open the subject naturally. I was eager to open diplomatic negotiations on my country's behalf, but I was restrained by a desire to miss no advantage through a too brusque and undiplomatic beginning.

Presently, while we continued our gay conversation, and our consumption of the delicacies of Lady Slasher's abundant table, there was a commotion at the entrance to the grounds. The crowd parted with looks of curiosity and a young man, looking warm and dusty, came with rapid strides in our direction carrying a port-folio under his arm. The laughing counte-nance of the Marquis settled into its official ex-pression of gravity as he took the portfolio and said:

" Well, Jamison ? "

The young man uttered half a dozen words in a low voice.

" Will you excuse me ? " said His Lordship, with a smile. " It is a dispatch of some im-portance which demands an immediate reply. Do not go "—I was rising to leave the table— " I've a lot of questions to ask you yet."

With that the Marquis of Silsbury, upon whose shoulders much of the future weal or woe of England rested, rose and walked toward a deserted portion of the grounds, conversing earnestly with the messenger.

This incident, which seemed of such trivial importance on its face, was observed with evi-dences of extraordinary interest by the English portion of the assemblage. The foreigners paid only passing attention to it, but Her Majesty's subjects, gathering into groups, appeared to be discussing it with a gravity bordering upon anxiety. Mr. Squibs came up drawing a note-book from his pocket. He asked a dozen questions all in a breath, glancing at me almost pleadingly.

"You were here when the messenger arrived. What did His Lordship say? What did he do? Where is he now? What did the messenger say? What did he do? Where did he go? Has he gone yet?"

"No. Yes. No. We don't know. We wouldn't tell if we did," laughed the Honorable Mrs. Pebblestone in the journalist's face. "One would imagine you had been taking lessons from the Yankees, Mr. Squibs."

"In my opinion that's what we'll all be doing presently," said the journalist.

"Be patient," said I; "the Marquis has withdrawn with the messenger for a few minutes to answer an important dispatch. He'll be back presently."

"An important dispatch?" repeated Mr. Squibs. "Ah, I thought as much. I'd lay a guinea to half a crown it's by cable from Hong Kong."

"Hong Kong?" I said, eagerly. "Isn't that the nearest cable communication with Manila?"

"Yes; and also with Great Britain's agents entrusted with the duty of watching Russia's secret dickerings with Li Hung Chang," said the journalist.

" Ah, the Marquis will not be back as soon as we expected," said the Honorable Mrs. Pebblestone, with her glass leveled in the direction His Lordship had taken on leaving us.

Every one in our neighborhood seemed to be looking in the same direction—that is, all the Englishmen. But there was nothing more remarkable to be seen than the Prince and the Marquis walking about together, while the messenger followed at a short distance.

" I win," said Mr. Squibs, excitedly. " It's the Chinese frontier."

" Dear me," said I, disappointed, " I was in hopes it was the Philippines."

" There's no hurry about the Philippines, with your Dewey still on the bridge of his flagship. We'll look into that matter later—perhaps. But the Chinese frontier is our own affair—and it's urgent."

" Does it mean war between England and Russia ? " I asked, hopefully.

" It does unless Russia keeps her hands off."

" In case of war so far away from home," I said, insinuatingly, " England will need help, won't she—more battleships, and expert gunners ? "

"That's the idea, exactly," said Mr. Squibs. "If we go to war with Russia on the Chinese frontier question there's no telling what may happen. The alliance will probably go to pieces, and there'll be the devil to pay generally."

"Oh, well, don't worry," said I. "By that time we will have whipped Spain and will come over and help you out."

"I say," said Mr. Squibs, with a grin, "you tell that to the Marquis of Silsbury."

At this moment His Lordship seemed to be noticing with annoyance the interest his movements had created in the minds of Lady Slasher's guests. He said a word or two to the Prince, who smiled, and both joined the Duchess of Edgecombe, who was walking with Lord Dunstable. After a short conversation Lord Dunstable came over and said to me loudly enough for every one within a dozen yards to hear:

"Miss Casino, Her Grace, the Duchess of Edgecombe wishes to present you to the Prince."

Mr. Squibs put up his note-book. "It can't be the Chinese frontier after all," he said, and walked away, evidently much relieved.

"It is the Chinese frontier," I said to myself, "and my presentation to the Prince is the Marquis of Silsbury's cute way of making Lady Slasher's guests forget all about his dispatch."

As I took Lord Dunstable's arm and hastened to obey the Duchess of Edgecombe's flattering command I noticed that all eyes were upon me. The Marquis of Silsbury's dispatch was already forgotten.

It was worth all I had suffered that afternoon to see among the envious glances turned upon me that of Countess Pipedreme, her enameled features twisted into an expression of mingled hatred, malice and consternation which I shall never forget.

The Duchess of Edgecombe left the Prince's side, and, advancing a few steps to meet us, placed her arm about my shoulders as though I had been her own daughter. I caught one more glimpse of Countess Pipedreme's wrathful countenance as she turned and quickly left that part of the grounds. Her face was drawn and haggard; she seemed to have grown years older.

"My dear," the Duchess was saying, "the Prince has heard you sing at the theatre. His Royal Highness admires you greatly. But his

"The Prince had heard me sing."—Page 244.

mind is occupied with very serious matters to-day, so do not feel hurt if he seems to lack the interest in you which I assure you he feels."

The Prince smiled and held out his hand as the Duchess mentioned my name. There was just then another surprised movement of the crowd at the entrance to the grounds, but I was too perturbed over the great honor being conferred upon me to notice that a second messenger was approaching, this one wearing the Prince's livery.

"Very glad, I'm sure," said His Royal Highness. "How do you like England?"

Before I could command my scattered wits to make an intelligible reply to this important question, the Prince had bowed his apologies and turned to receive what the messenger had brought.

The Marquis of Silsbury offered me his arm, as much as to say: "Shall we leave His Royal Highness free to issue his commands?"

As by an inspiration I saw that the time was now ripe for my entrance into the arena of diplomacy. I took the Marquis' arm, and as we strolled among the shrubbery I felt my brain clear and my heart beating strong and steadily—the brain and heart of a victor!

CHAPTER XVIII

MY DIPLOMATIC RELATIONS

"WELL," said the Marquis, smiling quizzically down upon me, "how do you like England? I will take great pleasure in reporting your answer to His Royal Highness."

"I think I answered that question, with more energy than courtesy, perhaps, upon the occasion of our first meeting, My Lord."

"I remember perfectly. You find it difficult to give your entire confidence to a nation that does not appreciate its own Dickens."

"Since then," I hastened to reply, "I've been thinking over what Your Lordship said."

"Ah! Your memory, then, is better than my own."

"Your Lordship made quite a little speech. It contained both commendation and rebuke. I remember it word for word. You said: 'My dear young lady, you will think better of us. I hope to live to see the day when America and England do stand shoulder to shoulder, for civilization and humanity, as you well express

it, against the rest of the world.' Then came
Your Lordship's rebuke : 'It is a pity that you,
who have such clear perceptions of what is
natural, and what is calculated to most benefit
humanity, should not bend your talents toward
their realization—instead of allowing yourself
to become incensed over small differences of
temperament.'"

" Whew! Did I say all that?"

" Every word of it."

" And you've been thinking it over?"

" It has never been out of my mind."

" And with what result?"

" Your Lordship's rebuke struck home. Why
shouldn't I love England? Isn't she of my own
flesh and blood?"

" By the same token," said the Marquis,
" why shouldn't you indulge in small family
quarrels with her—about Dickens, for example?
I dare say you have little differences with your
own sisters—perhaps, even, with your mother.
Most people do."

" The rebuke was just and I have profited by
it," I said; then, looking the Marquis squarely
in the eyes, I inquired, pointedly: " Was Your
Lordship equally in earnest when you said that
you hoped to live to see the day when England

and America would stand shoulder to shoulder
for "—

"Softly, softly," broke in the Marquis of
Silsbury, with a comically apprehensive glance
at a party of guests strolling near. "Softly, I
beg of you. Just now I saw you being inter-
viewed by Squibs of the *Gazette.* What I said
was not for publication."

"Why not?" I asked, boldly.

"What if the public mind is not yet ripe for
that sort of talk? Seventy-six and Eighteen-
fourteen are not so very far in the background,
you know. Who among us has not yet forgotten and forgiven? That is the question."

"Small family quarrels, Your Lordship."

The Marquis threw up his hands with another comical gesture as I quoted from his own
lips.

"We have forgotten—we, the disobedient
children; it is unworthy of you, the parent, not
to forgive."

"Come, now," said His Lordship, stopping
short and looking down upon me reflectively,
"would you have England and America enter
into a treaty of alliance?"

"No," I answered, with emphasis.

"No?"

"Certainly not."

"Dear me, dear me," said His Lordship, looking quite perplexed. "We have commercial treaties, a treaty on the fisheries question "—

"Father and son may contract to exchange the product of their labor," I interrupted with warmth; "but whoever heard of father and son signing an agreement to defend each other's life and property?"

"Good," said the Marquis, frankly. "Exactly the argument I've used all along."

"In the present instance," I continued, eloquently, quite forgetting that I was talking to the craftiest statesman in Europe, "the life and property of the father is in greater need of defence than those of the son. America's only entanglement is with Spain. Who doubts what the result will be? England, on the contrary, on whose possessions the sun never sets, is threatened everywhere. She is threatened even by those whom she had compelled to bind themselves to her in writing. These documents would be the first to turn to ashes in the conflagration which will result from the first match accidentally ignited—or," I added as His Lordship's messenger showed his face for an instant as though to determine whether he was wanted, "when Russia actually enters China by the back door she has opened at such vast expense."

His Lordship gave me a queer look. "Haven't you missed your vocation, Miss Casino? Really, the stage is not worthy of such talents as yours."

"How else would I have been able to meet Your Lordship?" I retorted.

The Marquis reflected a moment and then said :

"And do you really think our lusty son, America, would hasten to his parent's, England's, defence in her hour of need?"

"Why not? It would be a natural and filial act—particularly as the parent would have made in the meantime overtures for a reconciliation."

"Overtures? What's that?" demanded His Lordship, turning upon me sharply.

"Of course," I answered, composedly, "in all family quarrels it is the place of the elder to first hold out the hand of peace."

His Lordship doffed his hat and made me a low bow. "My dear young lady, your argument for your side of the general proposition is complete. It is unanswerable. If you can dispose of the details as readily, as convincingly, you've a better head for statecraft than any of

us. Proceed; I listen with the deepest interest, I assure you."

"I am very grateful, My Lord. I had not
hoped to interest you; only, perhaps, to accidentally let fall a word that would suggest to
Your Lordship the natural and logical course
for England to pursue in her relations with the
United States from this on. A child might do
that. The simplest way is the best, for you are
dealing, as you have just admitted, not with
the representatives of the people, but with the
people direct. Have you any doubt that Your
Lordship and the President of the United States
are of the same mind concerning the matter?"

"What desperate advantage do you purpose
taking of me if I make that important admission?" demanded the Marquis.

"Then we are agreed on that point," I went
on, calmly. "Now as to the people. Possibly
Your Lordship may not be aware that the people of the United States are bursting with
pride over the recent achievements of their
brave sailors?"

"I can understand that that must be so."

"That we are dying to have our courage
and our strength acknowledged and proclaimed
everywhere?"

"That is natural."

"And that especially we thirst for that recognition which is the sweetest of all—parental approval. We want the people of England to say: 'Bully boys! We're proud of you!'"

"From all accounts that is exactly what the people of England are saying," admitted the Marquis of Silsbury.

"Then there's nothing more for me to say," said I.

"Eh? What's that?" The Marquis planted his feet solidly in the path and confronted me.

"Your Lordship is the voice of the people," I said. "Now we are agreed what that voice is, all Your Lordship has to do is to make it heard."

"But the provocation—the shadow of an excuse"—

"If an honest desire to bestow praise where praise is due is not excuse enough," I interrupted, "there is the practical provocation of self-interest. The bad news you have just received cannot long be kept from the public, and"—

"Bad news?" repeated His Lordship, with an innocent expression: "what bad news?"

"The news from Hong Kong your messenger

brought a little while ago, about Russian aggressions in China "—

" What a lovely day it is," said the Marquis.

" All the English among Lady Slasher's guests are discussing it," I persisted ; " Mr. Squibs was sending a dispatch to the *Gazette* about it before your messenger had been here five minutes."

I thought for the fraction of a minute that the Marquis looked uneasy.   Presently he said, gravely:

" My news is bad for you—bad for the United States.   Austria is secretly sending large sums of money to Spain.   France and Germany note her action with approval.   There is a persistent effort to compel England to unite with the other Powers in forcing the United States to end the war with Spain."

" My Lord," I said, composedly, though the Marquis' words filled me with dismay, " the United States cannot be forced.   No one should know that better than Your Lordship."

The Marquis of Silsbury held out his hand. " You are a worthy representative of your country, my child.   I believe that you are discreet as well as wise.   I will therefore be honest with you.   It was the Prince's messenger that brought the news I have just given you.   As to that brought by my own messenger, you are right; it is from Hong Kong; the Russians are pushing their advantage to a point which England cannot tolerate."

"And the Powers have received the same news," I cried, eagerly. "They are taking advantage of England's necessity to turn her against the United States in Spain's behalf. Oh, if I could change places with Your Lordship for five minutes, I would, without touching pen to paper, without performing a single official act, teach Austria, Germany, France, and the rest of Europe such a lesson as will keep them henceforth well out of the range of American guns, glad to be permitted to manage their own affairs."

"I am open to conviction," said the Marquis.

"Say publicly what you said to me upon the occasion of our first meeting, and which I repeated to Your Lordship a moment ago. Say for yourself what the people are saying all over England. Say that the Anglo-Saxon race cannot be divided against itself."

"When and where will I find a natural opportunity to say such a thing?"

"Now. Here. You would have an audience the most cosmopolitan of its size ever assembled

in London. To-morrow morning all the world
would understand that the British Navy stands
guard over American rights among nations;
and that the new great sea power will not
prove ungrateful when England is threatened
in the East."

Before the Marquis of Silsbury could reply
the Duchess of Edgecombe had rejoined us.

"My Lord," said the Duchess, "the Prince
begs that you will advise him respecting the
dispatch he wishes to return by the messenger."

"Pardon, and—congratulations," said the
Marquis, smiling encouragingly upon me, as he
departed to answer the summons of His Royal
Highness.

The Marquis had hardly turned his back
when Mr. Squibs swooped down upon us, saying to the Duchess:

"Begging Your Grace's pardon, between
Royalty and Nobility the Press is being sacri-
ficed in the most abominable manner. I demand that Miss Casino be given up to me forthwith."

"Take her, if she's willing," laughed the
Duchess.

Having already assigned to Mr. Squibs, in
my mind, the important task of giving publicity

to such fruit as might be borne by my diplomatic relations, I welcomed the journalist's proposition. Leaving the Duchess, we returned to the neighborhood of the main refreshment table.

By this time the agitation of the English portion of Lady Slasher's guests seemed to have been communicated to all the others. All eyes were turned on the Prince and the Marquis, who walked about, conversing earnestly.

"Something is going to happen," said Mr. Squibs; "I can feel it coming. What were you and the Marquis talking about so earnestly?"

"Our conversation was strictly confidential," I said, "except that I suggested to His Lordship what a fine thing it would be if he would make a speech."

"I say, there's an idea," said Mr. Squibs, becoming quite excited. "Excuse me for one moment."

The journalist got up and joined a group of young Englishmen, to whom he said something which seemed to please them mightily. Then he rejoined me and said:

"That was a good stroke of business. By jove! We haven't long to wait, either. The

Prince and the Marquis are coming this way.
Ps-s-t, ps-s-t!" The journalist seemed to be
issuing some sort of command to his fellow con-
spirators. They responded shortly by taking
off their hats and shouting:
"Long live the Prince of Wales!"
The Prince bowed and smiled. Instantly
people began to gather from all parts of the
grounds.
"Marquis of Silsbury!" shouted the young
men. "Speech! Speech!"
Believing that the psychological moment had
arrived I began clapping my hands with all my
might. Mr. Squibs followed suit. The Honorable Mrs. Pebblestone, raising her glass,
glanced at the gathering multitude and began
to clap her hands also. Presently the hand
clapping became general. At a smiling gesture
from the Prince the Marquis of Silsbury raised
his hat and bowed to the crowd where it was
thickest.
"He's going to do it," said Mr. Squibs, excitedly. "What the deuce have I done with
my note-book. By jove, I've lost it!"
This calamity seemed to paralyze all the
journalist's faculties. But the sound of the
Marquis' voice galvanized them into instant

action. Mr. Squibs, with a muttered word of apology to me, tore open his white waistcoat and began scribbling little curves, dashes and pot hooks like mad up and down his shirt front.

Lightly and wittily, yet with an undercurrent of earnestness which could not be mistaken, the Marquis began a eulogy of the Anglo-Saxon race. Some Americans divined what was coming and began cheering.

"It's coming," said Mr. Squibs, as he hastily sharpened his pencil.

" What is coming ? " I asked.

" The Marquis' long contemplated unofficial suggestion of a tacit alliance between England and the United States. I was right about the dispatch after all. It was from Hong Kong. It is high time Russia, and the rest of the world should know where England stands. Excuse me."

The cheering having subsided the Marquis resumed and Mr. Squibs went on decorating his shirt front. The interest of the crowd was intense. The Marquis was making identically the same argument I had used a few minutes before. It seemed to me wonderful that I should actually have had a hand in bringing this thing

about. Every moment His Lordship was interrupted by applause which was no less hearty on
the part of the English than of the Americans.

" By jove ! This is history," said Mr. Squibs,
his pencil flying faster and faster.

I shall not attempt to describe the enthusiasm
with which Lady Slasher's guests received the
Marquis' peroration. It was couched in almost
the exact words which, at our first accidental
meeting, had launched me on my diplomatic
career. The Americans flung their hats into
the air and shook hands with the English
guests. The Prince patted the Marquis smilingly on the shoulder, and all the titled personages present deluged him with congratulations.

As for Mr. Squibs, we saw no more of him
that day. He caught the first train for London,
and long before the *Gazette's* presses were ready
to flood London with the great news, the pot
hooks on Mr. Squibs' shirt front had been
translated into cable messages that were in the
hands of half the editors in America by the
time Lady Slasher's guests had departed.

Twelve hours later all the world knew that
England and the United States understood
each other; that the enemies of one might expect to have to reckon with the other; that

there would be no outside interference in our war with Spain.

The Marquis of Silsbury's speech is already history, though history is silent respecting the part I played in the matter. Whether or not I am entitled to any credit for the part I played I am entirely satisfied to leave to the intelligent judgment of my readers.

CHAPTER XIX

I DECIDE NOT TO BECOME A MARCHIONESS

PRUE had been cross with me all the evening. While dressing me for the third act her conduct, considering her position, became scandalous. Finally I was compelled to have it out with her.

"I am not conscious of having committed any crime," I said, taking the brush from Prue's hand and proceeding to arrange my own hair; "my conscience is clear; really I don't look upon my life as having been lived in vain. If your opinion is to the contrary, for heaven's sake speak up. Don't stand about glowering at me as though I were a murderess."

"If this keeps up," said my companion, gloomily, "we shall have to take a larger house."

"If what keeps up?"

"This affair with Lord Dangerford."

"If you have an 'affair' with Lord Dangerford, Prue, I'd advise you to drop it. If you mean to insinuate that I have an affair with anybody, Lord Dangerford not excepted, you are wasting your breath."

"Another dray load of African plunder came this morning," growled Prue. "There is a stack of heathen fighting tools, spears and such like, that half fills the dining-room. There's a rhinoceros horn in the front hall that everybody falls over, an umbrella stand made out of an elephant's foot there's no place for except in the parlor, not to mention the skins of wild animals and the cooking utensils of savages strewn about so thick that you can't see the carpet. Either we must take a larger house or have an auction sale."

"You may look for a larger house, then," said I, "and let us hear no more about it. I appreciate these attentions on the part of Lord Dangerford most highly. I regard them in the light of the highest tribute which London has paid to my qualities as an artist. Nothing that Lord Dangerford has sent me is unworthy of a place in the British Museum."

Whatever rejoinder Prue had in her mind was denied expression by the explosive entrance of Tommy Atkins, who said, as she plunged head foremost into the room:

"Mr. Squibs has great news; he wants to know if he may come in?"

My third act toilet being now practically complete, the journalist was invited to enter.

"Mr. Squibs," I said, gayly, "I hope you properly appreciate the privilege of being allowed to call upon a diplomatist of my standing in her dressing-room—a privilege which only yourself, the American Friend and Lord Dangerford "—

"Speaking of Lord Dangerford," interrupted Mr. Squibs, "there is no such person. The old Marquis of Tidewater died a week ago. The title and the estates have descended to his grandson."

"And is Countess Pipedreme already a Marchioness?" I enquired. "Or will she wait until after the funeral before seizing her prey?"

"Good," laughed the journalist; "then I am the first to bring you the news after all. I was half afraid some one else had already had that honor. Countess Pipedreme is—ahem—is no longer in society."

"What do you mean by that?"

"It appears that the Countess and Dangerford had some sort of a quarrel at Lady Slasher's Garden Party, in which Dangerford's guardian, the Marquis of Silsbury figured, and "—

" The Marquis of Silsbury Lord Dangerford's guardian?" I exclaimed, beginning to see the solution of a great mystery.

" Yes.   His Lordship and the old Marquis of Tidewater—an eccentric old fellow who buried himself in the country a dozen years ago—were college chums.   Tidewater made Silsbury trustee of his estates, and executor of a will in which there was some sort of stipulation respecting the lady Dangerford should select for his wife. It has always been understood that Silsbury enjoyed large powers in this respect, and that Countess Pipedreme had convinced him of the superiority of her claims."

" Ah!" said I, more light breaking in upon me.

" The Countess always took particular pains to convince Silsbury that she was the only woman Dangerford had ever bothered his head about.   Until you came upon the scene at Lady Slasher's the Marquis had never seen Dangerford assert himself with respect to any other woman.   Perhaps you noticed something? There was talk of a scene in which you figured."

I felt my cheeks burning, so I merely nodded, and Mr. Squibs went on:

"At any rate, the Marquis took a great fancy to you, as everybody knows, and the Countess had tantrums all the rest of the afternoon. London hasn't seen her since."

"Will London be able to survive the loss of Countess Pipedreme?" I asked.

"Probably," laughed the journalist, "considering that the Earl of Drippingeaves"—

"The Earl of Drippingeaves missing, too? Then I was not mistaken after all."

"What did you see? What have you heard?" demanded Mr. Squibs. "The *Gazette's* information is only fragmentary, as yet."

"Countess Pipedreme and the Earl of Drippingeaves got lost among Lady Slasher's shrubbery," I said. "Walking with the American Friend, I came upon them suddenly. They were much confused."

"Then our correspondent at Havre was not mistaken," said Mr. Squibs, with satisfaction.

"You mean that?"—

"Countess Pipedreme and the Earl of Drippingeaves have eloped."

"Poor Drippingeaves!" said I.

Whereupon Mr. Squibs, much elated, took his leave.

As Tommy Atkins and I left my room to be ready for the rise of the curtain on the third act we nearly ran into Lord Dangerford—now the young Marquis of Tidewater—who was standing in the wings.

"Good evening," said the Marquis. "The manager said I might bring around the news. The Marquis of Silsbury's speech at Lady Slasher's has had the most extraordinary effect. There is no more talk about interference between the United States and Spain. In diplomatic circles it is taken for granted that England and the United States, in this affair at least, are to be considered as one nation."

At this good news Tommy Atkins danced a few steps to the accompaniment of swishing skirts, winked wickedly at His Lordship, and ran away, leaving us together quite alone.

"There's something else I've been wanting to say for a long time," began His Lordship in his hesitating way, "only I couldn't seem to find the opportunity."

"And I, My Lord, I feel that I have never properly acknowledged your many kindnesses. Believe me, my gratitude is too deep for words."

" Winked wickedly at His Lordship."—Page 266.

"On the contrary, Miss Casino, the obligation is all on my side. Before I met you I had a positive distaste for society; I cared only for my guns and the wild life of the jungle. Now I feel that with your help I can do what my late guardian, the Marquis of Silsbury, so earnestly desires me to do—remain in England, look after my estates, take my seat in parliament. Excuse me if I am too abrupt. I am not used to expressing my thoughts in words. Miss Casino, I have called to beg you to marry me —to ask you to become the Marchioness of Tidewater."

So completely was I taken by surprise that I was unable for a moment to even properly acknowledge the great honor bestowed upon me. I could think of myself only as a poor singing girl, standing there in my stage clothes, insignificant, almost laughable. So without thinking, I blurted out:

"Do I look like a Marchioness?"

His Lordship smiled at me reproachfully.

"Many a Duchess would exchange her title for your beauty."

Though I knew that I must send His Lordship away, I could not help asking:

"But what of Countess Pipedreme?"

"Poor Countess! I fear she is altogether lost. But I beg you to believe that it is not wholly my fault."

"My Lord," I said, "your conduct at Lady Slasher's was noble. I shall always love you for it."

No one was near us. I allowed the Marquis to touch my hand with his lips.

"I owe it to you," he went on, "to explain my relations with Countess Pipedreme. My youth was spent mostly in the country. The Countess was the only woman of society I met. She appealed to my boyish fancy. My grandfather was pleased. I promised to marry her. Except for our quarrel at Lady Slasher's—and its sad consequences for the Countess "—

"Do not reproach yourself on Countess Pipedreme's account," I interrupted; "it was already known that she was unworthy of you."

"So I have heard. Poor Countess!" Then His Lordship looked at me with real trouble in his honest eyes and asked:

"Am I to blame? Should I have protected her against "—

"My Lord," I hastened to say, "I have never known you to do anything, never heard of your doing anything, that was not honest, manly,

noble. I am proud—I shall always be proud—
to be your—friend."

"Nothing more?" I was sure His Lordship
lost color as he asked the question. "Do you
mean that you are going to send me back to
the jungle with my guns?"

"The English girls are lovely," I said with
enthusiasm. "Those in your own station in
life are divinely beautiful and charming. You
have but to choose among them"—

The curtain was up; my cue was imminent.
I gave the Marquis of Tidewater my hand.

"Be my friend," I said. "I love too many
to think of marrying."

"Too many!"

"My heart is full of them. I love them. I
yearn for them. I dream of them. They wear
the blue jackets of our navy. They stand behind our guns at Manila, at Santiago. I adore
them. I pray for them. Oh, My Lord, I am
hopelessly American. Forgive me."

His Lordship's face was now quite pale. He
touched my hand and turned away.

"Good-bye."

"Good-bye." And he was gone.

Then came my cue, from the orchestra, and
the applause with which these generous Lon-

doners greeted it nightly.   As I responded I fitted the inspiring notes to their words—the noblest couplet ever penned by a patriot—singing in my heart:

> The Star Spangled Banner, oh, long may it wave
> O'er the Land of the Free and the Home of the Brave!

THE END.

www.ingramcontent.com/pod-product-compliance
Lightning Source LLC
Chambersburg PA
CBHW060607030726
47498CB00005B/1581